THE PERFECT LOOK

CUL DE SAC (Book #3)
SILENT NEIGHBOR (Book #4)
HOMECOMING (Book #5)
TINTED WINDOWS (Book #6)

KATE WISE MYSTERY SERIES
IF SHE KNEW (Book #1)
IF SHE SAW (Book #2)
IF SHE RAN (Book #3)
IF SHE HID (Book #4)
IF SHE FLED (Book #5)
IF SHE FEARED (Book #6)
IF SHE HEARD (Book #7)

THE MAKING OF RILEY PAIGE SERIES
WATCHING (Book #1)
WAITING (Book #2)
LURING (Book #3)
TAKING (Book #4)
STALKING (Book #5)

RILEY PAIGE MYSTERY SERIES
ONCE GONE (Book #1)
ONCE TAKEN (Book #2)
ONCE CRAVED (Book #3)
ONCE LURED (Book #4)
ONCE HUNTED (Book #5)
ONCE PINED (Book #6)
ONCE FORSAKEN (Book #7)
ONCE COLD (Book #8)
ONCE STALKED (Book #9)
ONCE LOST (Book #10)
ONCE BURIED (Book #11)
ONCE BOUND (Book #12)
ONCE TRAPPED (Book #13)

ONCE DORMANT (Book #14)
ONCE SHUNNED (Book #15)
ONCE MISSED (Book #16)
ONCE CHOSEN (Book #17)

MACKENZIE WHITE MYSTERY SERIES
BEFORE HE KILLS (Book #1)
BEFORE HE SEES (Book #2)
BEFORE HE COVETS (Book #3)
BEFORE HE TAKES (Book #4)
BEFORE HE NEEDS (Book #5)
BEFORE HE FEELS (Book #6)
BEFORE HE SINS (Book #7)
BEFORE HE HUNTS (Book #8)
BEFORE HE PREYS (Book #9)
BEFORE HE LONGS (Book #10)
BEFORE HE LAPSES (Book #11)
BEFORE HE ENVIES (Book #12)
BEFORE HE STALKS (Book #13)
BEFORE HE HARMS (Book #14)

AVERY BLACK MYSTERY SERIES
CAUSE TO KILL (Book #1)
CAUSE TO RUN (Book #2)
CAUSE TO HIDE (Book #3)
CAUSE TO FEAR (Book #4)
CAUSE TO SAVE (Book #5)
CAUSE TO DREAD (Book #6)

KERI LOCKE MYSTERY SERIES
A TRACE OF DEATH (Book #1)
A TRACE OF MUDER (Book #2)
A TRACE OF VICE (Book #3)
A TRACE OF CRIME (Book #4)
A TRACE OF HOPE (Book #5)

THE PERFECT LOOK

(A Jessie Hunt Psychological Suspense Thriller—Book Six)

BLAKE PIERCE

BLAKE PIERCE

B lake Pierce is author of the bestselling RILEY PAGE mystery series, which includes sixteen books (and counting). Blake Pierce is also the author of the MACKENZIE WHITE mystery series, comprising thirteen books (and counting); of the AVERY BLACK mystery series, comprising six books; of the KERI LOCKE mystery series, comprising five books; of the MAKING OF RILEY PAIGE mystery series, comprising five books (and counting); of the KATE WISE mystery series, comprising six books ; of the CHLOE FINE psychological suspense mystery, comprising six books; and of the JESSE HUNT psychological suspense thriller series, comprising seven books (and counting).

ONCE GONE (a Riley Paige Mystery—Book #1), BEFORE HE KILLS (A Mackenzie White Mystery—Book I), CAUSE TO KILL (An Avery Black Mystery—Book I), A TRACE OF DEATH (A Keri Locke Mystery—Book I), and WATCHING (The Making of Riley Paige—Book I) are each available as a free download on Amazon!

An avid reader and lifelong fan of the mystery and thriller genres, Blake loves to hear from you, so please feel free to visit www.blakepierceauthor.com to learn more and stay in touch.

Table of Contents

CHAPTER ONE

Gordon Maines looked at himself in the hotel bathroom mirror and couldn't help admire what he saw staring back at him.

For a third-term city councilman considering a run for mayor, he exuded the confidence of a man who regularly bent the system to his will rather than the other way around. Beyond that, he just looked good.

He was approaching fifty, but thanks to a comprehensive regimen of skin care (with a small Botox assist), he told himself that he could still pass for forty. His wavy hair was still more pepper than salt. His skin was tan but not in an unhealthy-looking way. He still looked fairly dashing in a suit, though he wasn't wearing one now.

In fact, all he had on at the moment was a white undershirt and a pair of boxer briefs. And soon those would be gone too. As he popped the little blue pill into his mouth and took a swig of brandy, he considered what was waiting for him in the other room.

This was far from the first time he'd done this, but the woman he'd brought up to room 1441 of the Bonaventure Hotel may have been the most impressive yet. The purple dress she wore was sophisticated and stylish, but form-fitting enough to suggest at the bounty hidden underneath. Part of him wondered what she was doing in this line of work. She was gorgeous enough to be a model or actress, or at the very least a porn star.

But Gordon didn't spend too much time worrying about the girl's long-term employment prospects. Right now she was here and she would do whatever he wanted, even if he had to pull money from the slush fund he kept on the side, the one he used so his wife wouldn't stumble across his various peccadilloes.

He stepped out into the well-appointed room with its latte-tinted walls adorned in modern art, thick carpeting, and marble-topped dressers, and was surprised to find the bed unoccupied. For a second, thinking she'd absconded with the first half of her payment, he started for the door.

"Where you headed, big boy?" a voice purred from the corner of the room.

He glanced in that direction and saw her, the girl who'd demanded they not use names, sitting in a high-backed chair in the corner near the window, wearing only a black bustier and hipster panties. Her proportions were almost Barbie-like, something he intended to investigate in greater detail soon.

Her long blonde hair cascaded down, approaching her elbows. Her skin wasn't nearly as tan as the average California girl, giving her a delicacy and sophistication that seemed somehow exotic in this land of sun and surf. Her eyes were a bright blue, reminiscent of the Caribbean waters where he'd spent his honeymoon.

Gordon immediately shook that thought from his head and focused on the creature in front of him.

"I'm headed in your direction," he answered, certain he sounded suave.

"Before you do, I poured you another drink," she said, nodding at the counter above the mini-bar as she took a sip from a glass of her own. "I decided not to wait."

"Rude," he said, pretending to be offended as he grabbed the glass.

"Hopefully I can make it up to you," she said, her tone lilting with playfulness.

"I'm sure I can think of something," he replied before taking a swig. "Mmm, is that brandy?"

"You mentioned that it was your favorite when we were downstairs," she said.

"Wow, you paid attention," he marveled, before taking another glug. "Most girls in your line of work don't pay attention to anything other than the cash."

"Are you saying I'm not the first gal you've been with?" she faux pouted, sticking out her lower lip with such ferocity that he could barely contain himself.

This girl is good.

He reminded himself to add a little something extra if the rest of her efforts delivered on the performance so far.

"Why don't you take off your shirt and stay awhile?" she suggested, standing up and letting him drink her in fully.

"Don't mind if I do," he murmured, pulling his shirt up more clumsily than he would have liked.

In fact, as he lifted it over his head, he lost his balance and stumbled slightly. Luckily he landed on the bed, where he managed to finally wrangle the shirt off, even if he felt his hair getting messed up in the process. He was irked at his lack of smoothness but reminded himself that the blonde girl didn't really care.

She was standing over him now, a hint of a smile on her face. Maybe she found his awkwardness endearing.

"Clumsy much?' she cooed as she walked over to the chair he'd rested his slacks on, sliding on what looked like plastic gloves as she went. He watched her move but found himself struggling slightly to focus.

She pulled his wallet out of his back pocket and slowly flipped through it, pulling out all his cards and dropping them in a small plastic bag. He tried to prop himself up on his elbows to get a better view but his arms weren't responding to orders from his brain.

"Heyyy..." he tried to say, though his tongue felt unwieldy in his mouth.

The girl glanced over at him and smiled sweetly.

"Feeling relaxed?" she asked as she walked back over to her purse and dropped the plastic bag in it.

Somewhere in the back of his brain, it occurred to Gordon that the girl might be trying to rob him. He also thought she might have slipped something into his drink. It was time to put a stop to this.

With all the strength he could muster, Gordon pushed himself up into a sitting position. His head lolled lazily atop his neck as he tried to fix his gaze on her.

"You...stop," he tried to shout, though it came out as more of a mumble. It felt like he had a pile of marbles in his mouth.

As she walked over to him, he began to see double, then triple, unable to discern which girl was the real one.

"You're cute," the middle image said as she pushed him back down on the bed. "Shall we begin?"

She climbed on top of him and straddled him. Gordon's body was heavy and numb and he could barely feel her weight. He saw that she still wore the plastic gloves.

In his increasingly hazy mind, an alert sounded. This was more than just a drugging and robbery. Something about the casual, unhurried way the woman was moving suggested she wasn't just out for his money and possessions. She was enjoying herself. The way she shimmied up his torso reminded him of a snake slithering slowly up the branch of a tree.

"What . . . doing?" he managed to garble.

She seemed to understand him perfectly.

"I'm delivering on a promise," she relied breezily, as if she were answering a question about the weather.

Gordon stared into her blue eyes and saw that all the earlier playfulness had disappeared from them. Now they were icy and focused. He knew he was in trouble. The realization sent a sudden surge of adrenaline through his system, which he used to push himself up from the bed.

He expected to pop up and have the woman fall off him to the floor. But he had barely risen six inches when she pushed him back down, using only an index finger to the chest to force him back into his original position. Then she leaned down so that their faces were only inches apart. Her hair fell into his eyes but there was nothing he could do about it.

"This is it for you, Gordon," she whispered in his ear. "Any final words?"

His eyes, the only part of him he still seemed able to control, opened wide. "Arghh . . ." he sputtered.

"Never mind," she said brusquely, cutting him off. "I don't really care."

Gordon watched as she sat up straight again and wrapped her hands around his neck. He couldn't actually feel her squeezing his throat but knew she must be because breathing suddenly became challenging. His eyes started to bulge and felt like they might pop out of his skull. He desperately tried to gasp for air but couldn't seem to gather any into his chest. His vision blurred. His tongue darted around as if searching for any oxygen it could draw in. But nothing worked.

The last thing he saw before his vision went dark was the woman above him, staring at him intently as she strangled him. She was still smiling.

CHAPTER TWO

Jessie Hunt sat nervously in the booth at Nickel Diner on South Main Street, only two blocks from LAPD Central Community Station.

Though the person she was meeting would not care at all about her appearance, she wanted to make a good impression. In general, she deemed herself fit to be seen. Her green eyes were clear and her shoulder-length brown hair looked shinier than usual. She'd made sure to put on her most professional blouse and slacks before work today, along with flats that didn't accentuate her already regal five-foot-ten frame. She doubted anyone looking at her today would mistake her for a model, as sometimes happened. But just weeks from her thirtieth birthday, she knew she could still turn heads when it served her purposes.

All things considered, she thought she was doing pretty well. After all, it was just seven days ago that she'd been drugged by a murder suspect and had her stomach pumped. In the time since, after she was released from the hospital, she'd been mostly holed up at her apartment, under the care and protection of Detective Ryan Hernandez.

Ryan had insisted on staying with her until she'd regained her strength. So, for the last week, he'd been sleeping on the pull-out sofa in the living room and making most of her meals. Jessie had deliberately chosen to simply accept the help and not read too much into the actions of the man who was her sometime case partner and sometimes more.

Typically after extended medical time off, Jessie would have gone into work along with Ryan first thing to have her sign-off meeting with LAPD Captain Roy Decker. But today was unusual. She had decided to have a little meeting of her own, before the captain started placing rules and limits on her once she started work again.

While Jessie Hunt was a criminal profiling consultant for the Los Angeles Police Department and not an actual police officer, Captain Decker was still her immediate supervisor, and violating his orders could have serious repercussions. But if she just happened to meet with someone and have an informal discussion about an ongoing investigation *before* getting Decker's orders, well, that could hardly be held against her.

It was for that reason that she sat in the crowded diner at 7:30 a.m. waiting for the arrival of a man she'd only spoken to occasionally and almost always while battling nerves. She nibbled on her toast and sipped her second cup of coffee, well aware that she probably should have stopped after one. He walked in just as she put the mug down on the table.

Garland Moses glanced around the diner, spotted Jessie, and headed toward her. At seventy-one years old, with leathery skin, unkempt white hair, and bifocals that looked about to topple off the front of his nose, he didn't draw the attention of any of the customers he passed. None of them had any idea that they were in the presence of perhaps the most celebrated criminal profiler of the last quarter century.

Jessie couldn't blame them. The man seemed to cultivate an air of slovenliness. He shuffled toward her, seemingly oblivious to the shirttails sticking out above his rumpled corduroys and the stains on his oversized maroon sweater vest. His gray sports jacket, which hung off him like he was a coat rack, looked like it might swallow him whole.

But if one paid closer attention, other things became clear. Behind the thick glasses, his sharp eyes darted around quickly, taking in his surroundings in an instant. Though his hair was disheveled, he was crisply shaved without a stray piece of stubble. His teeth were still sparkling white and in perfect condition. His fingernails were neatly trimmed and the shoelaces on his well-worn loafers were tied in tight double bows. Garland Moses projected the slapdash look of a Columbo-style senior citizen. But as Jessie knew well, it was all an act.

Moses had been solving some of the hardest murder cases in the country for over forty years. He did it first as part of the FBI's celebrated Behavioral Sciences Division based out of Quantico, Virginia. Then, in the late 1990s, after twenty years of seeing the worst humanity had to offer, he retired to sunny Southern California.

But within months of his arrival, he was courted by the LAPD to serve as a profiling consultant. He agreed, with several conditions. First, he wouldn't be a formal employee so he wasn't subject to the rules and regulations of the department and could come and go as he pleased. Second, he got to pick his own cases. And most importantly to him, he didn't have to adhere to any dress code.

The department eagerly agreed. And despite his outwardly gruff demeanor or, as one officer called him, "a taciturn, short-tempered asshole," they never regretted it. Ensconced in his isolated, broom-closet-sized office on the station's second floor, Moses went about his work, where he could be counted on to solve at least three or four high-profile cases a year, typically ones that stumped everyone else.

For reasons Jessie had never understood, Garland Moses seemed to like her, or at least not outwardly object to her existence, which was pretty much the same thing for him. He'd even given her occasional advice on a few of her cases from time to time.

And though he'd never acknowledged it, she had learned that his recommendation had been instrumental in getting her admission into the vaunted, ten-week FBI Academy, which she'd completed just last year.

The highly selective program brought in the cream of the crop from local police departments to train them in the latest FBI investigative techniques. It was usually only available to seasoned detectives with decorated records. But Jessie, a relative rookie, had somehow been admitted. While there, she not only got to learn from instructors at the world-famous Behavioral Sciences unit, she also underwent intense physical training that included weapons instruction and self-defense classes.

Without question, her success at solving multiple high-profile murder cases, not to mention foiling an attempt on her own life by her ex-husband, had played a role in her admission. But of greater significance was almost certainly the good word put in on her behalf by multiple high-level L.A. law enforcement officials, Moses among them.

As he sat down across from her, Jessie felt certain that he could already sense the purpose for her appeal to meet with him early in the morning outside of work. Despite her nervousness, it was almost a relief. If he could already guess what she wanted, she could dispense with all the niceties, persuasion, and flattery her imminent request would typically require. He was here after all. That meant he was at least mildly interested.

"Good morning, Mr. Moses," she said as he settled in across from her.

"Garland," he replied in his signature raspy growl as he waved at the waitress for a coffee. "This better be good, Hunt. You were very cryptic on the phone. I don't like upsetting my morning routine. And you've definitely upset it."

"I'm pretty sure you'll find the shakeup worthwhile," she assured him before deciding to simply launch in. "I need your help."

"I figured. No one asks to meet with me to discuss china patterns, much to my chagrin," he said, straight-faced.

Jessie decided to take his crack as a good sign and played along.

"I'm happy to do that later, Garland, if you've got a hankering. But for now, my interest is less in tableware and more focused on serial-killing child abductors."

The server, who had just walked over with her coffee pot, gave Jessie a stunned stare. A cherubic forty-something blonde with "Pam" on her name tag, she quickly recovered, glancing away and filling up Garland's mug.

"I'm listening," Garland said after the server left, "as apparently was Pam."

Jessie decided not to ask how he knew the woman's name when he'd never looked up at her. Instead she launched into her pitch.

"I'm sure you're aware that Bolton Crutchfield is still on the loose and that just last week, he kidnapped a seventeen-year-old girl named Hannah Dorsey."

"I am," he said, offering nothing further.

He didn't need to. One didn't have to be a celebrated criminal profiler to know about the monstrous history of Bolton Crutchfield, who had murdered dozens of people in brutally elaborate ways and who had recently escaped from a psychiatric prison.

"Okay," she continued. "You may also know that I have a bit of history with Crutchfield—that I interviewed him over a dozen times when he was held at the NRD psych prison, where he told me that my good ol' pops, the serial killer, Xander Thurman, was his mentor and that they'd been in communication."

"I knew that too. I also know that, despite his admiration for your father, when it came time to choose between you, he warned you about the threat from your father, potentially saving your life. That must complicate your feelings toward him."

Jessie took a long sip of her coffee as she pondered how to respond.

"It did," she finally conceded, "especially since he made it clear that he intended to leave me alone from now on and pursue other interests."

"A détente of sorts."

Pam tentatively returned to take Garland's order.

"I'll have what she's having," he said, nodding at Jessie's toast. Pam looked disappointed but said nothing and retreated to the kitchen.

"Right," Jessie said. "Of course, I was reluctant to take the word of a vicious killer that he was going to live and let live. And then he took the girl."

"That bothered you," Garland noted, stating what he knew to be obvious.

"It did," Jessie said. "This was a girl I found being held by my father in a home with her adoptive parents. He was torturing her. She barely survived, as did I. The people who raised her didn't. So when, only weeks later, Crutchfield kidnapped her and killed her foster parents, it felt..."

"Personal," Garland completed her thought.

"Exactly," Jessie said. "And now, after a week of forced leave, a week in which Hannah has been in Crutchfield's clutches, I'm returning to work today."

"But there's a problem," Garland said leadingly, hinting that Jessie should cut to the chase. So she did.

"There is. The FBI has been assigned the case. I know that when I walk through the police station doors, I will be expressly prohibited from participating because of...my personal connection. But, knowing my own nature after nearly thirty years on this planet, there is no way I'm going to be able to just put it out of my head and go about my normal business. So I thought I'd enlist the assistance of someone who isn't beholden to the regulations that are about to be handed down to me."

"And yet," Garland said as his toast arrived. "I get the distinct feeling that I'm not your first choice for this task."

Jessie had no idea how he could have known that but didn't try to deny it.

"That's true. I wouldn't normally ask a celebrated profiler emeritus to do me a solid if I could avoid it. I particularly don't like asking them to do the dirty work of trying to discreetly suss out what's going on in someone else's investigation. But unfortunately, my first choice is unavailable."

"Who is that?" Garland asked.

"Katherine Gentry. She used to head up security at the NRD prison. We became friends during my many visits. But once Crutchfield escaped and multiple guards were murdered, she was fired. Since then, she's become a private investigator. Kat's new to the gig but she's good at it. I used her for something recently."

"But..." Garland pressed.

"But she's in the middle of another case that involves a lot of out-of-town surveillance so she doesn't really have the time. Besides, I thought this might be a little too raw for her, considering her connection to Crutchfield. I think she might be too close to it."

I see," he said, with a mischievous tone. "So you're concerned that a person might not be able to objectively assess the situation because of her personal connection to it. Does that description apply to anyone else you know?"

Jessie looked at him, well aware of the point he was making. Of course, if he knew just how personal this case was for her, he would likely be even more concerned. Then a thought occurred to her, one that might make him reevaluate how he looked at the circumstances.

"You're right," she said. "I'm not objective, more than you know. You see, Garland, what only a half dozen people in the world know is that Hannah Dorsey's father was Xander Thurman. She's my half-sister, something I discovered less than a month ago. So I'm definitely not objective about this."

Garland, who was about to take a sip of coffee, paused briefly. Apparently he still had the capacity to be surprised.

"That is a complication," he acknowledged.

"Yes," she said, leaning forward intently. "And I'm pretty confident that Crutchfield took her in order to mold her into a serial killer like my father and himself. That was what my dad was after with me. When I rejected him, he tried to kill me. I think Crutchfield is trying to pick up where Thurman left off."

"What makes you think this?" Garland asked.

"He wrote me a postcard that basically laid it out. And then he left a message in blood on the foster family's wall that reiterated the point. He's not being subtle about it."

"He does seem to be rubbing it in," Garland conceded.

"Right," Jessie said, sensing that he was warming to her plea. "So I willingly admit that I'm not exactly level-headed about this. And I get why Captain

Decker would refuse to allow me near the case. But like I said, I know myself. And there's no way I can just pretend a serial killer's not out there trying to turn my half-sister into his own personal Mini-Me. So I figured I'd turn to someone who could be more rational to keep tabs on the case and give me updates. Otherwise I'm going to go crazy. And it needs to be someone who can access the info but isn't bound by all the LAPD prohibitions."

Garland leaned back in the booth and pushed his glasses up away from his nose. He seemed lost in thought.

"Garland," she said, her voice a hushed whisper. "Bolton Crutchfield is trying create a monster just like him and he's doing it to a traumatized girl. That's bad enough, even if she wasn't my only living relative, a sister I've barely gotten to know. But he's doing it intentionally to toy with me, another in his endless sadistic games. I understand what's going on. I'm clear-headed about this. But if you think that understanding the situation means I'm going be able to steer clear because of a directive from my supervisor, you're sorely mistaken. If you say no, I'm going to pursue this myself, regardless of the consequences. I'm asking for your help, partly because you're better at this than me. But partly to save me from myself. I don't want to be dramatic and say my future is in your hands . . . But my future is in your hands. What do you say?"

Garland sat silently for a moment. Then he leaned in, about to answer. Suddenly Jessie's cell phone rang. She glanced down. It was Ryan. She sent it to voicemail and looked back up at the old man in front of her. Then she felt a buzz. Looking down, she saw a text from Ryan that said simply "911—pick up." A second later the phone rang again. She picked up.

"I'm in the middle of something," she said.

"There's been a homicide at the Bonaventure Hotel," Ryan said, "Decker assigned us. He said he's postponing our meeting with him and he wants us there ASAP. I'm driving over now to pick you up. I'll be out front in two minutes."

He hung up before she could reply. She looked over at Garland.

"I just got called to a murder scene. Detective Hernandez is on his way here to get me. I need a decision. What do you say, Garland?"

CHAPTER THREE

Jessie gripped the car's grab handle for dear life.

Ryan had turned on the siren and was tearing through the downtown streets, making sharp, sudden turns. Apparently the media had already been tipped off about a dead body in the fancy hotel and was forming a crowd outside. He wanted to get there before the scene got too chaotic.

Jessie was silently grateful that she'd stuck to toast for breakfast as she was tossed around in the car. Despite being discombobulated, one thing stuck with her. Garland Moses had said yes.

That meant that, if she could force herself to make the most of his involvement, she didn't have to spend every spare moment freaking out over Hannah's disappearance. There was now someone looking into it whom she trusted to make some headway, someone who would actually update her on the status of the case. To remain sane, she had to allow that to play out and not fixate on it every second.

Just as important, if she was going to be of any use in this Bonaventure case, or any future one, she had to have a clear head. She owed it to whoever the murder victim was in that hotel room to provide her most cogent, uncluttered analysis. As if he were reading her mind, Ryan spoke up.

"This wasn't my idea."

"What do you mean?" she asked.

"I thought we should ease back into work with at least a day or two of boring paperwork catch-up. But Captain Decker insisted on sending you out."

"That doesn't sound like him," she pointed out.

"Normally, no," he agreed. "But he was pretty explicit about wanting to assign you a case immediately to keep you occupied. He doesn't want you anywhere near the Dorsey case and he figured the best way to prevent that is to keep you busy."

"He said that?" Jessie asked.

"Pretty much. In fact, I think he wanted me to convey that to you, kind of like a warning."

"Okay, noted," Jessie said, debating briefly whether to tell Ryan about her meeting with Garland Moses.

Ryan knew that Hannah was her half-sister but not much more. Furthermore, she hadn't informed him of whom she had met with or why. He seemed to assume she was meeting with Kat Gentry and she hadn't corrected his impression. She was concerned that the more he knew about her efforts to learn about Hannah's case, the more vulnerable position he would be in professionally. She didn't want him to have to lie on her behalf to the boss if the issue came up.

Then again, not telling him felt like a personal betrayal of sorts. She glanced over at Ryan Hernandez, two years her senior, and quietly asked herself what she owed him. After all, while he was a detective and she was a profiler, they worked most cases together and were informal partners, even if it wasn't official.

Beyond that, over the last few years, their relationship had evolved from purely professional to professionally friendly, to genuine friendship, and now to something else. Ryan's wife had filed for divorce a few months ago after six years of marriage and, after some awkward verbal dancing, Ryan had recently confessed to Jessie that he was interested in her as more than just a partner.

She had felt the same way for some time but never acted on it. She'd found him attractive ever since she'd first encountered him, giving a guest lecture at a class she attended. That was even before she learned of his impressive pedigree as a detective with an elite unit of LAPD's robbery-homicide division called Homicide Special Section, or HSS. HSS dealt with homicide cases that had high profiles or intense media scrutiny, often involving multiple victims or serial killers.

All that only enhanced the already dashing figure he cut. Ryan was six feet tall and two hundred pounds of street-hardened muscle. And yet, underneath his short black hair, his brown eyes exuded unexpected warmth.

Now, with only their own mountains of personal baggage to prevent them from taking the next step, they were feeling each other out. There had been one kiss but nothing more. To be honest, Jessie wasn't sure if either of them was ready for more.

"Tell me about the case," she said, deciding to hold off on telling him about the Garland Moses meeting, at least for now.

"I don't know much yet," Ryan said. "The body was discovered by housekeeping in the last hour—a male, forty-something, naked. Wallet was empty—no identification, credit cards, or cash. Initial cause of death seems to be strangulation."

"Can't they ID him by checking who booked the room?"

"That's a little weird too. Apparently the card that was used to hold the room is registered to a shell company. And the name on the register is John Smith. I'm sure it will get unraveled but right now we're dealing with a John Doe."

They arrived at the massive Bonaventure Hotel, with its multiple towers and famous exterior elevators, the ones made memorable in the movie *In the Line of Fire*. Ryan flashed his badge to get past the police barricade and pulled up near the loading dock entrance.

A uniformed officer met them and led them to the freight elevator and from there, to the massive central lobby. As they walked through it to get to the main bank of elevators, Jessie couldn't help but be overwhelmed by the size and number of atriums and crisscrossing hallways and stairwells. It was as if the place had been specifically designed to confuse.

She trailed behind Ryan and the officer, taking her time, allowing the complications of the morning to fall away as she focused in on the task at hand. Her job was to profile this crime, to determine potential perpetrators. And that meant staying aware of the surroundings in which the crime had taken place—not just the room but the hotel as well. It was possible that something that happened out here may have impacted the events in that room. She couldn't ignore anything.

They passed a group of tourists excitedly heading for an exit in attire that suggested they were going to a famous amusement park. Just beyond them, in a circular, open bar called the Lobby Court, several men in suits were getting an early start on their drinking. A few burly men in identical blue blazers wandered around, wearing earpieces, clearly security. Jessie couldn't decide whether they were intended to be genuinely discreet or just to give that surface impression.

As they reached the elevators, one of the blazer guys joined them and silently waited for one to arrive.

"How's your morning going?" Jessie asked him chipperly, unable to treat the guy with the solemnity he was clearly after.

He nodded but said nothing.

"You finishing your shift or starting it?" she pressed as her tone became more severe, annoyed at his lack of responsiveness.

He looked at her, then at Ryan, who stared at him coldly, and reluctantly replied.

"I started at six. We got the call from housekeeping at seven," addressing the topic she was clearly hinting at.

"Why did housekeeping go in the room so early?" Jessie asked. "Was there a cleaning request on the doorknob?"

"She said there was a smell coming from the room."

Jessie looked over at Ryan, who had a resigned expression.

"Sounds like a fun way to start the morning," she said, reading his mind.

The elevator arrived and they stepped inside. The guard accompanied them to the fourteenth floor. As they shot up in the air, Jessie couldn't help but marvel at the view. The elevator faced the Hollywood Hills, and on this fairly clear morning, the white Hollywood sign gleamed back at them, seemingly close enough to touch. Griffith Park Observatory was nestled nearby at the top of a hill in the park. Various studio soundstages peppered the expanse in between, as did thousands of vehicles on the traffic-choked streets.

A soft ding brought her back into the moment and Jessie stepped out, following the guard and Ryan to the end of the hallway. They were only halfway there when Jessie got a whiff of what must have captured the maid's attention.

It was the smell of putrid, bacteria-laced gases in the victim's body building up and leaking out, often with equally foul-smelling fluids. While it was always unpleasant, Jessie had gotten somewhat used to it. She doubted a housekeeper would be as familiar or as comfortable with it.

An officer waiting outside the door recognized Ryan and handed him and Jessie plastic slippers as he lifted the police tape so they could enter. To her admittedly petty satisfaction, the officer refused to allow the hotel security guard entry.

Once inside, she stood by the door and took in the scene. There were several CSU techs taking photos and fingerprinting the room. Multiple small indentations in the carpeting had been noted and marked with evidence numbers.

The body lay on the bed, naked, bloated, and uncovered. The initial description of the victim seemed accurate. He appeared to be in his forties. As Jessie got closer, it was clear that he had indeed been strangled. Blueish-purple finger marks covered his neck, though notably, there were no indentations or cuts that might suggest nails digging in.

The man was in decent shape if you ignored the bloating. He was clearly well off, with recently manicured fingernails, a hair transplant that had been painstakingly done to give him a smattering of gray amidst his black hair, and some craftsman-like Botox injections near the eyes, mouth, and forehead.

His socks, now straining at the excess fluid building up at his ankles, clung mournfully to his feet. His shoes rested by the side of the bed. His clothes—comprised of an expensive-looking suit, boxers, and a T-shirt, were folded neatly over a desk chair.

There were no other obvious personal materials in the room—no luggage bag, no extra clothes, no watch or glasses by the bedside. She glanced in the bathroom and saw the same thing there—no toiletries, no used towels, nothing to suggest that he'd spent much time in the room at all.

"Cell phone?" Ryan asked the officer standing in the corner.

"We found it in the trash can," the CSU investigator told him. "It was smashed but the tech team thinks it's salvageable. The SIM card was still inside. It's being transported to the lab now."

"Wallet?" Ryan wondered.

"It was on the floor by the bed," the investigator said. "But it had been picked clean. Almost everything potentially identifiable was gone—no credit cards or driver's license. There were a few photos of kids. I guess they could eventually be used to establish identity. But I suspect the cell phone will yield results quicker."

Jessie stepped closer to the body, making sure to avoid all the evidence markers on the carpet.

"No obvious defensive wounds," she noted. "No scratches on his hands. No bruising on his fingers."

"Hard to imagine he'd just lie there and take a choking, unless it was part of a sex game. Of course, we've seen that before," Ryan said, referring to a complicated case involving S&M that they'd solved recently.

"Or he could have been drugged," Jessie countered, pointing at the empty glass lying on the desk near another evidence marker. "If something was slipped in his drink, he might not have been able to put up a fight."

"So I guess we're ruling out suicide," Ryan said as he moved closer to the body.

"If he did this himself, that would be a pretty impressive accomplishment," Jessie said.

She watched as Ryan's expression changed from amusement to curiosity.

"What is it?" she asked.

"I think I recognize this guy."

"Really?" Jessie said. "Who is he?"

"I'm not sure. I think he might be a local politician, maybe on the city council?"

"We should check his photo against local pols and other officials," Jessie suggested.

"Right," he agreed. "If that bears out, then we can't rule out a political motivation."

"True. It could be that someone was unhappy with a vote he'd recently cast or was about to. Of course, one would think that just showing him photos of himself drugged and naked in a hotel room would have been equally effective."

"Good point," Ryan acceded. "Maybe it was intended as a message to someone else."

"Also a possibility," Jessie said as she looked around the room for something she might be missing. "But I would have thought that as far as messages go, two bullets to the back of the head would have been more impactful. I think we need to find out who this guy is before we can draw any real conclusions."

Ryan nodded his agreement.

"Why don't we go down to the front desk," he said. "Let's see what they can tell us about John Smith."

The desk agent who had checked in "John Smith" of City Logistics had ended his shift at six a.m. and had to be called back in. While they waited for him to arrive, Ryan instructed the security office to pull up all video footage from the time of check-in and any key card swipes of the dead man's hotel room door.

Jessie sat in the lobby with Ryan and waited, watching the ebb and flow of the hotel routine. Some folks were checking out. But most were either tourists milling about or people in business attire headed out for what looked to be "titans of industry"–type stuff.

She knew the desk agent had arrived the second he walked in. Dressed in blue jeans and a casual shirt, the twenty-something, acne-faced kid looked like he'd been woken from a deep slumber and barely had time to throw on clothes, much less brush his hair. He also had another characteristic that seemed to envelop him like an invisible coat: fear.

Jessie tapped Ryan and pointed at the guy. They got up and reached him just as he approached the desk. He waved down a manager, who motioned for him to go to the end of the counter away from the guests.

"Thanks for coming in, Liam," the manager said.

"No problem, Chester," the kid said, though he looked put out. "You said it was urgent. What's this all about?"

"Some folks have a few questions for you," Chester said, following Jessie's instructions not to be specific about the reason Liam was being called in.

"Who has questions?" Liam asked.

"We do," Ryan said from behind him, startling the young guy and making him jump a little.

"Who are you?" Liam asked, trying to sound tough and failing.

"My name is Ryan Hernandez. I'm an LAPD detective. This is Jessie Hunt. She's a criminal profiler for the department. Why don't we go somewhere private where we can talk freely?"

For half a second, Liam looked like he might run for it. Then he seemed to get his bearings.

"Yeah, okay, I guess."

"There's a small conference room at the end of that hall," Chester the manager said. "It should afford you some privacy."

When they got into the conference room with the door closed and everyone had taken their seats, Liam seemed to tense up again. It might have been having two law enforcement officials staring at him, or not knowing why he was being questioned, or the strange white noise being pumped into the otherwise silent room. Jessie suspected it was a combination of all of it. Whatever the reason, Liam couldn't contain himself.

"Is this about the beer cases?' he blurted out. "Because I was told it was extra stock and would be thrown out so it was no big deal if I took them."

"No, Liam," Ryan said. "It's not about cases of beer. It's about a murder."

CHAPTER FOUR

Liam's jaw dropped open so far that Jessie worried it might unhinge from his face.

"What?" he asked when he was finally able to speak again.

"A guest was murdered here last night," Ryan said. "And it appears that you checked him in, though there's some confusion about that. We were hoping you could clear it up."

Liam gulped hard before responding.

"Of course," he said, apparently happy that he was no longer under suspicion about the beer.

"Yesterday evening at nine thirty-seven, you checked in a man identified only as John Smith. The card associated with the transaction was listed under a company called City Logistics, which appears to be a shell company."

"What does that mean?" Liam asked.

"It means," Ryan said, "that the company is owned by another company which is owned by another company, all with multiple people listed as executives, each of whom seem to be lawyers known for setting up shell companies."

"I don't get it," Liam said, looking genuinely confused.

"Liam," Jessie said, speaking for the first time," this means that the person who gave you the credit card didn't want his real name connected with booking the room, so he used this company card with the complicated history. That's probably why he signed in as 'John Smith.' And since the card was never charged, I'm assuming he paid for the room in cash, correct?"

"That sounds like someone who checked in last night," Liam conceded.

"But here's what I don't get," Jessie pressed. "Even if he paid in cash, the card would have been charged for incidentals like the small bottle of brandy from the mini-bar. How did that get paid for?"

"If we're thinking of the same guy," Liam said timidly, "it might be because he slipped me two hundred dollars and said any incidental charges for the room should be taken out of that. He also said that I could keep whatever was left over."

"How much was left over?" Jessie asked.

"A hundred eighty-four dollars."

Ryan and Jessie exchanged glances.

"That's a lot of money, Liam," Jessie said. "Why would John Smith leave you such a massive tip? And remember, right now you're just a potential witness. But if your answers end up being less than truthful, we might have to bump you up to suspect."

Liam didn't look like he wanted any part of that.

"Listen," he said, barely able to get the words out fast enough. "The guy never said anything obvious. But he hinted that he might have a friend visit him that evening and the less of a paper trail there was, the better it would be for him. He wanted to keep things off the books, you know?'

"And you were okay with that?" Ryan pushed.

"It was two hundred dollars, man. Times are tight. Even if he had gotten five mini-brandy bottles, I'm still bringing home north of a hundred bucks for doing nothing. Am I supposed to be the moral judge of whether some dude can use this hotel to meet up with his mistress? Worst-case scenario, he rips the room up and I have the corporate card on file in case of emergencies. I figured it was a no-lose situation."

"Unless he ends up naked and dead on the bed," Ryan noted. "That ends up being a loss for everybody, including you, Liam. Regardless of the whole beer case thing, I'd say you're going to need to dust off your resume."

A knock on the door prevented Liam from responding. It was Chester the manager. Ryan motioned for him to open the door.

"Sorry to interrupt," he said. "But security has pulled up the footage you were interested in."

"Perfect timing," Ryan said. "I think we're done here for now, right, Liam?"

Liam nodded, looking despondent. As Ryan and Jessie left the room, he tried to follow but the manager held up his hand for him to stay.

"I'd like you to stick around a bit longer, Liam," he said. "We have a few things to discuss."

※ ※ ※

Jessie put Liam's problems out of her head as she stood in the security office, leaning in behind the young woman operating the system so she could get a better look at the monitor. Ryan and another hotel manager stood next to her.

Just as Liam had described, the man booking the room handed him a card and a wad of cash. He was alone. As he waited for Liam to complete the transaction, he glanced around and seemed to nod at somebody off camera.

"Can you get a look at who he was motioning to?" Jessie asked the technician.

"I already tried," the woman, whose name was Natasha, said. "I looked at every camera shot in the area he was focused on. No one seemed to respond physically. In fact, no one seemed to even be looking in his direction."

Jessie found that intriguing but she said nothing for now. The man had clearly been nodding at someone. But that someone was aware enough to avoid being captured on camera.

Who would know those kinds of details?

"You have the hallway footage for the fourteenth floor?" she prompted.

Natasha pulled it up. The timestamp read 10:01 p.m. as the man walked down the hallway and entered the room. Jessie heard Ryan inhale sharply and looked over. He leaned in and whispered in her ear.

"Seeing the way the guy walked jogged something in memory. I just realized who he is. He *is* a politician. I'll fill you in when there aren't so many ears around."

Jessie nodded, curious. Natasha fast-forwarded through the footage of the hallway, stopping periodically when someone walked by. No one approached the man's room. But at 10:14, exactly thirteen minutes after the man had gone into his room, the elevator opened and a woman stepped out.

She was a statuesque blonde, with hair that cascaded down to the middle of her back. She wore huge sunglasses that obscured her features and a cinched trench coat with a high collar. She wandered down the hall, glancing at the room numbers before coming to a stop at the man's door. She knocked. It opened only seconds later and she stepped inside.

Nothing happened for the next thirty-one minutes. But at 10:45, the women exited the room and returned the way she'd come. This time she was walking toward the camera so Jessie could get a better view of her.

She still wore the sunglasses and coat. But even with them, Jessie could tell that the woman was well put together. Her cheekbones appeared sculpted by an artist. Her skin, even on this small monitor, looked flawless. And it was clear that underneath that jacket she had the kind of figure that could easily make a wealthy, horny man put his political future at risk.

Jessie noticed something else too. The woman seemed to be … strolling toward the elevators. There was nothing hurried about her demeanor. It was quite possible that only minutes earlier she had drugged and strangled a man to death. And yet nothing about the way she carried herself suggested any worry or anxiety. She looked confident.

And that's when Jessie became certain that they were dealing with something more than just a crime of passion or a robbery gone wrong. If it had been a physical encounter that went south, she would have looked much more harried and rushed. If it was a simple robbery, she could have been in and out of the room in less than ten minutes.

But she'd stayed a half hour. She'd lingered. She'd smashed his phone and taken all his cards, cash, and ID, even though she had to be well aware that his identity would be quickly uncovered. She'd even left family photos in the wallet.

Even more notably, she had apparently left no prints on anything in the room; not the glass, not any surface in the room, not the man's neck. This was the work of a woman who had carefully planned what she would do, who had taken her time, who had enjoyed herself.

CHAPTER FIVE

Jessie couldn't get the image out of her head.

As Ryan drove them to their next stop, she kept thinking back to the final footage that Natasha the security tech had shown them. Now that they knew what the woman looked like, she was able to scan through video from earlier in the night.

There was no recording of the woman arriving or leaving the hotel. But there was footage of her settling in at the Lobby Court—the very bar Jessie had noticed the men in suits drinking at earlier that morning.

She had arrived a little after nine p.m. and waited for fifteen minutes, sipping a drink she'd purchased with cash and drinking with leather gloves on. The thing that jumped out at Jessie was how relaxed she looked. She didn't have the bearing of someone who would murder a man less than two hours later.

Eventually her "date" arrived. He walked straight up to her as if they knew each other but strangely greeted her as if it was the first time they'd met. He ordered a drink of his own and sat down beside her. They talked for a half hour as he ordered two more drinks and she continued to nurse her first.

Around 9:50, he paid his bill and got up. Cameras tracked him to the bathroom and then the front desk. The woman stayed at bar a little longer to finish her drink, and then walked out of frame, not to be seen again until she got out of the elevator to go to his room.

"What are you thinking?" Ryan asked, interrupting her silent meditation.

"I'm thinking that we're dealing with someone who enjoyed what she did. And that makes me worry that she might do it again."

"Legitimate concern," he agreed. "Can I tell you what I'm worried about?"

"Please," Jessie said.

"I'm worried that this guy's wife is going to lose it when we tell her what happened."

Ryan was referring to the inevitable unpleasantness they were about to face. After they'd left the security office he'd told her who the dead man was: Gordon Maines.

When Ryan had called his suspicion in to the ME, they confirmed it for him. The victim was indeed Gordon Maines, a councilman representing Los Angeles's fourth district, an area that included Hancock Park and Los Feliz.

Ryan had finally remembered him because of his jaunty walking style. It was the same style he'd had when he'd come to the station once several years ago to dress down Captain Decker for not giving him enough officers for security at a neighborhood parade.

"'Jerk' is the kindest word I can think of to describe the guy," Ryan had said.

Jessie hoped he'd use more diplomatic language when they arrived at Maines's Hancock Park home to deliver the bad news to his wife, Margo. As he navigated the mid-morning traffic, Jessie's thoughts returned, despite her best efforts, to Hannah.

She wondered if Garland Moses was having any success determining how the investigation was going. Did the FBI have any leads on Bolton Crutchfield's possible whereabouts? Was Hannah safe? She was tempted to text him to ask and actually pulled out her phone before reminding herself it was a terrible idea.

First, it had only been a couple of hours since she'd met with him. Garland Moses might be the most decorated profiler in the country, but even he wasn't a superhero. Besides, if he had information, he would surely let her know. Radio silence likely meant there was nothing worth sharing.

Second, they'd agreed to only communicate verbally. Even though Captain Decker hadn't yet formally forbidden her from getting involved in the case, it was only a matter of time. Any record that showed she'd tried to get around that directive could put her career at risk and, as Garland had said, mess up her "sweet gig."

Still, it gnawed at her. Here she was, investigating the death of a man who clearly had several skeletons in his closet. Meanwhile, an innocent young girl was being held captive by a serial killer, simply because she shared the same DNA as another serial killer.

The frustration rose in her chest and it was all she could do to swallow it back down.

Garland Moses better find something soon. Because I don't know how much longer I can hold this in before it boils over.

When they pulled up to Gordon Maines's mansion in Hancock Park, Jessie wasn't surprised.

She already knew they were dealing with a man who was willing to book a $400 hotel room to cheat on his wife; a man who apparently had a credit card associated with a bogus company, a likely sign that his finances were sketchy too. And he apparently lived in a home no civil servant could afford unless he inherited it.

As they walked up the steps to the front door, Jessie reminded herself not to take her distaste for the victim out on his wife, who might think her husband hung the moon and was about to learn otherwise. Ryan rang the bell and they waited, both apprehensive about what was to come.

The door was opened by a petite, trim woman in her late forties. She was dressed in a tan business suit and her blonde hair was tied up in a bun. Despite her professional appearance, Jessie could tell she was in bad shape.

She had shadows under her eyes that couldn't be masked, even with heavy makeup, despite a valiant attempt. The eyes themselves were red, a sign of anything from lack of sleep to crying to drug use. None of the choices indicated anything good. She had a long run in her right stocking, which she apparently hadn't noticed, suggesting her thoughts were elsewhere.

"Can I help you?" she asked, her voice scratchy.

"Hi, are you Margo Maines?" Jessie asked gently.

"Yes," she said warily. "What's this about?"

Jessie looked at Ryan, who appeared ready to deliver the news they knew would break her. She'd seen him do it many times before and saw the same reaction now, a stiffening of his spine, as if preparing himself to accept the emotional blowback he was about to get. Suddenly, a wave of empathy rushed over her at the thought of how many times he'd been in this situation in his career. She felt a powerful urge to shield him from it this time and stepped forward slightly.

"We're from the Los Angeles Police Department," she said before he could get a word out. "I'm Jessie Hunt and this is Detective Ryan Hernandez. I'm afraid we have some bad news for you, Mrs. Maines."

Margaret Maines, or "Margo" as she was called in her husband's bio on the city website, seemed to know what was coming. She lowered her head as she reached out and gripped the doorframe. Ryan inched forward slightly just in case she collapsed.

Luckily, it wasn't necessary. She looked back up at them with a resolve that Jessie admired, though it appeared fragile.

"Let's go inside," Mrs. Maines said. "I think I'd like to sit down before you tell me anything else."

Jessie and Ryan followed her into the living room, where she sat on the loveseat and motioned for them to take the adjoining couch. Once they were all settled, she looked at them both and nodded.

"Go ahead," she said resignedly.

Jessie continued, not looking at Ryan to see if he was okay with her taking point.

"I'm afraid your husband has died, Mrs. Maines. His body was found this morning at a downtown hotel. His identity was recently confirmed."

Mrs. Maines nodded, took a deep gulp of air, and reached for a tissue. As she dabbed at her eyes, she replied.

"I knew something was wrong. He never came home last night. Sometimes he works very late. But he always calls. And he didn't pick up any of mine. I actually thought about calling the police. But then I pictured him sleeping in his office with his phone on silent or with a dead battery. I didn't want to overreact. I called the office this morning and they said he hadn't come in yet. I knew something was wrong. I was this close to calling."

"Why didn't you?" Jessie asked, keeping her tone non-accusatory.

"Gordon was very particular. He hated bad press. I could hear his voice in my head saying, 'If you call the police, it'll end up in the papers. It'll be on the news. My opponent in the next election will turn it into something nefarious no matter how innocent. There's no room for public relations mistakes in modern politics.' He was very big on avoiding bad press. Now I wonder if I could have prevented this by calling."

Jessie thought it was ironic that a guy who was concerned about PR was apparently carrying on some kind of tryst and bankrolling it with what appeared to be a slush fund. But she kept that to herself.

"Don't blame yourself, Mrs. Maines," Ryan said. "From what we can tell so far, it looks like your husband died last night. No call you could have made would have saved him."

She seemed to take some small solace from that, sighing deeply with something approximating relief. She appeared to be debating whether to ask her next question but finally just spit it out.

"How did it happen?"

Jessie, feeling only slightly cowardly, determined that Ryan's years of experience on the job might come in handy for this one and decided to let him answer.

"Maybe we save the details for another time, Mrs. Maines," he suggested gently.

The broken look on the woman's face was quickly replaced with a combination of irritation and resolution.

"Tell me the truth, Detective. It's clearly not just natural causes. I'm going to find out sooner or later. And I'd rather hear it first in the privacy of my own home than in some cold morgue surrounded by a group of strangers. I'll take two strangers over ten any day."

"Yes, ma'am," he said. "You're correct. It wasn't natural causes. I'm afraid he was strangled to death. The circumstances surrounding his murder are somewhat . . . salacious. Shall I go on?"

"Please," Mrs. Maines insisted, her voice flat.

"It appears that he was at the hotel for a rendezvous with an as-yet-unknown woman. We don't know her motive. We just know that he was likely drugged, then robbed and strangled."

Jessie watched as the woman's face hardened. She felt a twinge of anxiety as she wondered whether Margo Maines was going to blow up or break down. It turned out to be neither.

"I'm quite confident it was a drugging and robbery," she insisted crisply as she sat up straight. "There is no way Gordon would have gone willingly to a hotel room with some woman unless his clarity had been altered."

Jessie remembered the footage of the bar, in which Gordon had happily flirted for a half hour before going to book a hotel room, all without being slipped a thing. She wondered if she should burst his wife's bubble of certainty but decided that wasn't her job.

Another moment of moral cowardice.

"In any case," Ryan said in a "moving on" voice, clearly not wanting to challenge her either, "even though we have confirmation it's him, we'll need someone to come down to the medical examiner's office to formally identify the body. If you'd rather one of his staffers do that, we can accommodate your wishes."

"No, I'll do it," she said.

"Thank you," Ryan said. "There is one other thing. We don't have many leads on the woman we suspect of killing your husband. But she did take all of his credit cards and identification."

"What about his watch?" Mrs. Maines interrupted.

"What watch?" Ryan asked.

"He had a Rolex watch with his initials inscribed on the back."

"We didn't find it at the scene," Ryan said. "But we'll add it to the list of missing items."

"I gave him that watch for our tenth anniversary," she said, her thoughts clearly drifting back to that moment.

Jessie had an idea but decided to put a button in it for now. Reluctantly, Ryan pulled Maines back into the present.

"We'll do our best to recover it, ma'am," he assured her. "But regarding the credit cards, rather than cancelling them, we were hoping to track them in the hopes that we could catch her in the act of using one. She might also try to forge any number of documents using his ID. Would you give us permission to review his transactions and financial data to see if there are any anomalies?"

Mrs. Maines cast a skeptical eye at him, clearly aware that his request likely had an ulterior motive.

"That seems broad," she noted.

"It is," he admitted. "We want to cast as wide a net as possible so we don't miss anything. We can get a court order if need be. But that takes time and I worry she might slip through our fingers in the interim. But if you sign the releases now, we can get started immediately."

Mrs. Maines still looked somewhat unconvinced. But the way Ryan had framed it, saying no would look like she was hampering the investigation of her husband's murder. After a moment it became clear that she'd decided that whatever skeletons she suspected he was hiding would ultimately have to take a backseat to catching his killer.

"Give me the papers," she said roughly.

Ryan, who already had the envelope waiting, handed them over. Jessie saw him fighting the urge to smile and had to fight her own urge to kick him.

He was lucky that Margo Maines didn't know his expressions as well as she did. New widows don't usually appreciate self-satisfied smirks.

CHAPTER SIX

Jessie was getting frustrated with Ryan.

They were back at the station, sitting at their desks, rifling through confusing financial documents while they waited for the tech team to untangle the origins of "City Logistics" and where it got its resources. Captain Decker was at a meeting at headquarters, meaning Jessie had still managed to avoid the sit-down where he would inevitably warn her away from Hannah's case.

In the meantime, Ryan had floated the idea that Margo Maines was faking—that she had uncovered her husband's dalliance and hired a hit woman to take him out, either for revenge, the life insurance, or both. In fact, he seemed fixated on it.

"She just didn't seem credible to me," he insisted. "I don't buy her claim that Gordon had to be drugged to go up to a hotel room with another woman. You saw that footage from the bar. He was all in. Margo had to at least have a hint about his lecherousness."

"I'm sure she did," Jessie agreed, despite her agitation. "But that doesn't mean she took a hit out on him. Maybe she just wasn't comfortable acknowledging to two people she'd just met that she'd been looking the other way when it came to his bad behavior. Wives have been known to do that."

Jessie kept her voice steady so he wouldn't pick up on how raw this discussion still was for her. Her own ex-husband, Kyle, had cheated on her for months. And though the signs were all around her, Jessie had somehow managed to miss them.

In her more honest moments, she acknowledged that she might have intentionally ignored them because confronting them would have blown up her marriage and her life. Of course, that happened anyway when Kyle murdered his mistress, framed Jessie for it, and then tried to kill her too. But that wasn't the point here.

"Maybe she wasn't comfortable revealing she knew he cheated because she was embarrassed," Ryan conceded. "Or maybe she knew that admitting it would give her a motive."

Jessie didn't want to dismiss his theory. It wasn't crazy. And he'd been at this a lot longer than she had. But he seemed to be ignoring some other relevant details.

"Let me ask you this," she offered. "If this was a paid hit, why not go with the double tap to the head? It's much quicker and more surefire."

"Maybe Margo Maines knew the details would eventually come out. Her husband would be shamed and she'd be the martyred wife. She'd get sympathy galore and no suspicion."

"That explains it from her end but not the killer's," Jessie countered. "The woman who killed him took her sweet time. Even if she'd been tasked to make the scene look tawdry, she could have been in and out in less than fifteen minutes. She was there twice that long. She lingered. That's not the work of a professional. And she could have just drugged him and left it at that. A dead, naked, drugged-up politician found in a hotel room is embarrassing enough. Why the strangling too? No. This feels personal."

Ryan sat with that for a while. The argument seemed to make an impact. Jessie's frustration level dropped a notch.

"That's a good point. I hadn't thought of it from the killer's perspective."

"Yeah, well, you're not the profiler," she said, tweaking him slightly.

He flicked her off playfully. But a sudden flash in his eyes told her he had a new theory.

"What about this?" he began. "Maybe the woman *was* his mistress. It could be she didn't know he was married or maybe he'd promised he'd leave his wife for her. Either way, by last night she's discovered that he's stringing her along and she's pissed. So she decides to get a little revenge for herself. She kills him up close and personal. Then she gets everything: vengeance on the guy who used her, a chance to destroy his reputation and as a lucky strike extra, the wife loses her big-time important husband."

"I like that idea better than the other one," Jessie allowed.

Just then, Camille Guadino from the tech team walked over with some paperwork and a rueful smile. Fresh out of school, she was the rookie of the unit, assigned to the most mundane tasks.

"Uh-oh," Ryan said, looking at her. "Don't tell me you're going to give us actual evidence we'll have to follow up on instead of just spinning endless webs of theories."

"Sorry, Detective, but yeah," she said as she dropped a folder on his desk. "Real, fresh-brewed evidence coming your way."

"What have you got, Guadino?" Jessie asked.

"It took a while but we finally figured out what City Logistics is all about."

"Urban planning enthusiasts?" Jessie quipped.

"So close," Guadino replied. "It's a consulting firm that 'offers feedback and recommendations on urban improvement issues.'"

"What the hell does that mean?" Ryan asked.

"It means it's pretty much what you guys suspected. It's a shell company run by a lawyer owned by a shell company also run by a lawyer who's a partner in the same firm that represents a consulting agency that has done work for a strategist associated with—you guessed it—Gordon Maines."

"What does all that gobbledygook mean to us?' Ryan sked.

"It means that, via multiple cutouts, Maines had access to a corporate account with over two hundred eighty grand in it. And it looks like someone at an ATM located in the Bonaventure Hotel withdrew two grand in cash from that account at the time Maines was there."

Jessie and Ryan exchanged a look that acknowledged the theories they'd been discussing for the last ten minutes were now likely moot.

"What?" Guadino asked, sensing she was missing something. "Did I screw up somehow?"

"No, you're good," Jessie assured her. "Go on."

"Okay. We've been tracking all of his credit cards and haven't gotten any hits. I'm starting to doubt we will. Usually, these cards get used in the first hours after a robbery, before the victim discovers they're gone. Or in this case, before the body is found."

"Was that a joke?" Ryan asked. "Did you just make fun of a man's death for cheap laughs?"

"Uhhh . . ." Guadino started to sputter.

"I'm just screwing with you. That was a good one. Anything else?'

"Yes," Guadino said, dispensing with the humor and sticking to the facts. "The damage to his phone turned out to be minimal. We were able to get all his recent texts and a call log. It's in the folder. But he didn't make any calls or text anyone in the hour prior to withdrawing the cash."

"Thanks, Guadino," Jessie said. "We'll take it from here. You can go ahead and get back to working on your stand-up routine."

Guadino smiled sheepishly and left. When she was gone, Jessie looked over at Ryan.

"Are you thinking what I'm thinking?" she asked.

"That you could really go for a pastrami on rye right about now?"

"That too," she said, happy to embrace his attempts at levity, "but also that this woman isn't looking like a mistress at all. It sounds like Gordon was paying for his evening. I think we're dealing with a pro."

"I agree," he said. "That would explain her hanging out at a fancy hotel bar."

"Women sometimes hang out at bars, Ryan," Jessie chided. "It doesn't always mean they're prostitutes."

"I didn't mean it like th—"

"I'm just screwing with you," she said, grinning. "You're not the only one who can play that game. It does fit the profile. But it doesn't explain why there was no phone communication prior to their meet-up. If this was a first-time date, they'd need to nail down the particulars of when and where. But there's none of that."

"Right," Ryan said. "And he didn't look surprised to see her, which makes me think this wasn't the first time they'd met up."

"But if this was a regular thing, why did she wait until now to kill him? And why rob him if he was willing to pay upwards of two grand anyway?"

"Maybe she wanted to make sure he really had deep pockets and wasn't just fronting. Of course, once she knew, one would expect her to use those cards ASAP after she left him in that room. She had to know they'd be cancelled by the morning. But there's not a single purchase."

"I get the sense that this woman is too smart to use those cards," Jessie said. "She wore gloves the whole night. The scene was clean. She knew how to avoid the hotel cameras. Remember how there was no footage of her when he nodded at her in the lobby? She wouldn't be so sloppy as to risk using the cards and getting busted after the fact."

"Then why take them?" Ryan asked. "What's the point?"

"Maybe to make it harder to identify him? She took his license too and that doesn't make much sense. Or maybe just to humiliate him even more—to add insult to injury. I'm thinking that might be why she took the Rolex too. Not because it's worth so much money but because of the inscription. It had personal meaning and value to Maines. Taking it might have been a way of taking away the power that came with his identity."

"So you don't think she'd pawn it?"

"I didn't say that," Jessie said. "A pawned watch would take a lot longer to track down than credit cards. If there was anything she might sell, that would be it. It's a long shot but I think we should reach out to shops in the area."

"I'll have Dunlop look into it. He's on good terms with almost every downtown broker. If she tried to pawn that watch anywhere east of the 405 freeway, he'll know about it."

"Sounds good," Jessie said. "While you reach out to him, I need to check on something."

"You're not going to butt into the Crutchfield thing, are you?' he asked warily. "Just because Decker hasn't officially warned you off it yet doesn't mean he won't."

"No, Ryan," she snapped as she stood up. "I am not going to butt into the case. Have a little faith, why don't you?"

He raised his eyebrow skeptically as she got up and headed for the second floor. She gave him a mock offended scowl before turning toward the stairs.

I'm not butting into the case. I'm just going to ask a few questions.

She refused to address the question of whether there was any real difference.

CHAPTER SEVEN

Jessie was surprised at how nervous she felt.

She rarely visited the second floor of the station, which was used mostly for storage and administrative offices. In fact, as she walked down the long hallway, she didn't pass a single soul.

She stopped at the door to the tiny office marked with the simple nameplate "G. Moses" and knocked quietly. She heard a bit of paper shuffling from the other side and then what sounded like the crack of elderly kneecaps stretching out. The noise sent a shiver down her spine. A moment later Garland Moses opened the door.

"I lost," he said in his familiar rasp when he saw her.

"Lost what?" she asked, her blood pressure suddenly rising.

"I had the over in the over/under bet on whether you would pester me for the first time before or after noon. It's eleven fifty-six a.m. so I lost. I owe myself ten bucks."

Jessie was relieved that he was only mocking her and allowed herself a moment to breathe before responding.

"Well, hopefully you pay up quick. I hear your methods of collecting late payments can be rough. "

"You have no idea," Garland said, his mouth breaking into something close to a smile. "Let's just say there's forced Metamucil involved."

"Nice," Jessie said, gagging slightly. "So how much longer do I have to politely talk about your senior health routine before you fill me in on the situation?"

Garland half-smiled again. It seemed to be turning into a habit.

"Come in," he said, moving aside.

She took one step into the office before realizing she couldn't take another without bumping into his desk.

"I thought people were being sarcastic but this really did used to be a closet, didn't it?"

"I don't need a lot of room," he replied, closing the door and squeezing past her to get to the chair on the other side of his small desk. Other than that, a single chair for guests, a desk lamp, and a half-sized file cabinet, the room was empty.

"I guess when you only take on a few cases each year, you don't get drowned in paperwork."

"I liked to keep the paperwork to a minimum even back in my busier days. A cluttered desk means a cluttered mind."

"Confucius?" she asked teasingly.

"No, Moses, but not the bible one," he said. Before she could reply, he continued. "So on to your case."

"Yes?"

"I've got nothing."

"What?" she asked incredulously.

He seemed untroubled by her reaction.

"The truth is I haven't even tried yet."

"Why not?" she demanded.

"Think about it, Hunt," he said patiently. "I can't just walk over to the local FBI office, saunter in, and ask the assigned agents how their investigation is going, especially on the same morning the profiler most connected to Crutchfield returns to work. It will be obvious what I'm doing. They'll shut down. You'll get in trouble. And I'll lose my official status as 'grandiose emeritus.' That's no good."

"You make it sound impossible," Jessie protested. "No matter how you approach them, they'll have their guard up."

"Not necessarily, especially if I happen to be already enjoying my lunch at a joint I know they frequent. And if they join me because of the whole 'grandiose emeritus' thing, maybe they get to talking. Maybe they want to impress the old man and they spill a little more than they should. Maybe I seem disinterested so they tell me even more, to prove their mettle. Folks like to do that around me."

"Because of your 'grandiose emeritus' status," Jessie repeated.

"Now you're getting it," he said. "But no one's going to tell me a thing if I come out and ask them directly. They're FBI agents, not second graders."

"So why aren't you out having lunch?' she pressed.

"Because they don't usually show up at this place until around one. That's why I called the owner and told him to hold a table waiting for me at twelve forty-five—a booth in the back, with a little privacy and room for three."

"You've already done that?"

"I have."

"I'm sorry," Jessie said, impressed. "I shouldn't have jumped down your throat. It's just that Hannah's out there, with God knows what happening to her. I saw you hanging out here and it got me riled up. I shouldn't have made assumptions."

"I appreciate that, Hunt. And I don't blame you. An old guy like me, you'd be forgiven for thinking I completely forgot about our little chat this morning. But can I give you a piece of advice?"

"Of course," she said.

"You have to loosen your grip a little."

Jessie nodded.

"That's been challenging for me," she admitted.

"I get it," he replied. "I was the same way for a long time. But the thing is, with what we do, there's always going to be some bad guy out there. There's always going to be a victim in danger. There's always going to be a ticking clock. But if you've got the accelerator pressed to a hundred all the time, you're going to crash. It's inevitable. And then you're no good to anyone."

Jessie nodded. Everything he said resonated. Before she could admit it, he continued.

"I know it's not easy, and especially not now, when the person at risk is your own half-sister. But you have to hit the brakes sometimes. You have to find some kind of equilibrium in your life. Otherwise you will burn out. And people you could have saved will die. I'm not saying you shouldn't work hard. And I'm not saying you shouldn't care. But you have to find that line where you can do this job and still be a functioning human being. Otherwise you'll be miserable. You know what I mean?"

Jessie felt like she'd never better understood anything in her life.

"I do," she said simply.

"Good," he replied. "Then get the hell out of my office. I need to take a little siesta before lunch."

And with those words of wisdom still in her ears, she left him to his nap.

CHAPTER EIGHT

Hannah Dorsey reminded herself that she wasn't dead yet.

It might have seemed obvious, but this time a week ago, she couldn't be so sure. And every minute that she was alive meant she had a chance. At least that's what she told herself.

She knew it was around midday because of where the glimmer of window light shined on the floor in the basement where she was being held. For a while she thought she'd been moved out of California because she'd never seen a basement here before.

But the man—he had told her to call him Bolton—had explained that the former owner was an East Coast transplant who had demanded one be built in his new Southern California home, even if it didn't really make geological sense.

Bolton had explained a lot of things to her.

In the first few hours after he'd killed her foster parents and drugged and abducted her, he didn't do much talking. That was partly because Hannah was too drowsy to understand him at first. After that, her panicked screams made talking impossible.

But after about eighteen hours, she'd shouted herself hoarse. Beyond that, she was so wiped out from fear, adrenaline overload, and confusion that listening to the man's southern-inflected accent became almost a balm. If he was talking, he wasn't killing. So she was happy for him to talk away.

She imagined he'd be coming by to chat soon. He always brought her lunch around the time the light from the small window hit the middle of the room, which she estimated to be noon. She'd figured out a few other things in the week she'd been here.

First of all, she knew it had been about a week because she was able to scratch a notch for each day into the wooden post she was chained to with the spoon he left her. In fact, she was pretty sure it was Tuesday. She also knew they were somewhere isolated. Otherwise Bolton would have gagged her or at least boarded up the small window that offered her that shred of sunlight.

He clearly wasn't worried about someone hearing her calls for help or smashing the window and seeing her down here. Besides, she hadn't heard anything like a car driving by, a plane passing overhead, or an alarm going off in the distance.

At night, through the window's smeared dirty glass, she was able to see the flashing pink and blue neon sign in the far distance for a place called Bare Essence. The style of the sign suggested to her that it was probably a strip club. But considering she wasn't an expert on places like that, the information wasn't of much use.

She was also pretty sure he didn't want her dead, at least not yet. It wasn't for a lack of willingness to kill. Back at her foster parents' house, before he drugged her but after he gagged her and tied her up, he'd carried her quietly into the living room and sat her in the corner so she could watch as he killed them.

He hadn't done it stealthily. In fact, there was casualness to him throughout the ordeal. Her foster father was asleep in the easy chair and her foster mother was seated on the adjoining loveseat watching the TV.

Since they were facing away from him, he'd simply gone into the kitchen and come out with two knives, one a smaller serrated variety and the other a large carving knife. He gave Hannah a little wink as he walked around behind the couple and sat down next to Hannah's foster mother, a bland, gray-haired but generally decent woman named Caryn.

Caryn must have assumed it was Hannah and only glanced over after the show went to commercial. When she saw the strange man with the knife smiling beside her, she opened her mouth to scream. That's when he plunged it into the side of her throat.

She made an odd wheezy, gurgling sound, as if someone had let the air out of a balloon while underwater. Her foster father, Clint, who wasn't objectionable but clearly only participated in the foster process at his wife's behest, stirred slightly but didn't wake up.

As Caryn's blood spurted across the living room, some of it spraying on Bolton, he got up and wandered over to Clint. The man didn't react so Bolton grabbed the remote control and began turning up the volume until it was so loud Clint couldn't help but awaken.

"Too loud," he muttered grumpily.

When he didn't get any response, the man rubbed his eyes and looked at the screen. It was only then that he realized his view was blocked by a shortish, pudgy man with patchy brown hair and a double chin. Bolton smiled widely, revealing front teeth desperately in need of dental work, as several of them jutted in different directions. His bright, intense brown eyes never blinked.

Then, as if a starting bell had gone off at a horse race, he leapt forward and sank the carving knife into the center of Clint's chest. Hannah couldn't see her foster father's face, only the back of him as his body stiffened briefly and then sagged back into the chair. He never made a sound.

Bolton looked over at her and shrugged as if to say, "I thought there'd be more to it."

Hannah knew she should be freaking out. And she was sure that reaction would come. But in that moment after Caryn and Clint were butchered, she didn't have much of a reaction at all. She wished she could have but it just wasn't in her, not after everything else.

Only two months earlier, she'd gone through something equally traumatic. She and her adoptive parents had been kidnapped from their San Fernando Valley home and transported to a big mansion near downtown L.A. That time the perpetrator was an older man, likely in his fifties, and he was much less playful. Later she would learn that his name was Xander Thurman and that he was a notorious serial killer.

But at the time, all she knew was that she'd been brought to this strange house by this strange man. He tied her to a chair and made her watch as he proceeded to torture her adoptive parents. He left for a while before returning to finish what he'd started. Then a woman—Hannah later discovered she was a criminal profiler named Jessie Hunt—came into the house, apparently looking for him. He surprised and attacked her, knocking her out.

While she was unconscious, he strapped her arms to a ceiling beam. When she came to, he tortured her as well. The two of them engaged in a vicious verbal back and forth that was mostly lost on Hannah. Eventually, the woman's quick thinking gave her the upper hand, which led to a ferocious fight that left the man dead and the woman in awful shape.

Hannah managed to free herself and get help. She didn't remember much of the night beyond that, other than that the EMTs had to sedate her because she started to lose it. When she woke up, she was in the hospital. After questioning by multiple detectives, she was sent briefly to a group home and then to live with Caryn and Clint.

The next several months were a blur. She tried to go to school but found focusing difficult. The county got her a tutor to home school her and that went a little better. She cut her hair pixie-short so that when she looked in the mirror, she wasn't reminded of the girl from the family photos, the photos of a family that no longer existed.

It didn't really work. Her hair was still sandy blonde, her eyes were still green, and her long legs still made her look like a baby giraffe. She was still Hannah, whatever that meant.

Somewhere in that period, a detective came to follow up on the statement she provided the day after the attack. She repeated what happened, only this time it felt like she was reporting it from a distance, like she hadn't actually been a participant in the events that destroyed her family.

It was only then that she'd learned all the details about the man who'd killed her parents. Apparently this cop wasn't as fixated on protecting her emotional well-being as the others had been. He told her the man was Xander Thurman, a notorious serial killer responsible for dozens of deaths from the Midwest to California over the last quarter century. When she asked, he couldn't offer any explanation as to why he'd targeted her family.

Only a couple of days later Jessie Hunt showed up at her foster parents' house while she was lying in the porch hammock, reading *The Catcher in the Rye* for an English assignment. They had a weird conversation in which Hunt seemed to try to connect with her by comparing personal tragedies. Apparently Hunt's birth mother and her adoptive parents had all been murdered too.

And then, only days later, Bolton Crutchfield showed up to end her brief respite in purgatory, and introduce her to his own version of hell. It could have been worse, she told herself. He hadn't tried to touch her inappropriately. Other than drugging and chaining her to a wooden post, he hadn't harmed her. And after concluding that his attempts at conversation were genuine and not just a way to lower her guard before brutalizing her, she found him to be strangely entertaining.

The man had an oddly courtly demeanor for a killer and kidnapper. He reminded her of a cross between the Southern gentlemen from *Gone with the Wind* and the dad on that old sitcom her adoptive parents loved, *The Beverly Hillbillies*. And he was a pretty decent cook. Breakfast was often eggs and grits. Lunch was usually a sandwich of some kind. He was a big fan of something called a po'boy. Dinner varied among several meals he told her were staples from his Louisiana youth, including gumbo and étouffée.

Suddenly, she was ripped out of her thoughts by the sound of a door unlocking at the top of the wooden stairwell in the corner of the basement. She'd guessed right. It was lunchtime. The familiar sound of the door creaking open was followed by footsteps coming down the stairs, which groaned at the weight. Hannah found herself oddly worried that one would give out, sending Bolton crashing to the floor.

She told herself her concern was only that she'd be left helpless and chained up in an isolated basement, now without even sustenance to survive. But somewhere deep down, she feared she might be developing some warmth toward this genteel monster.

"I'm afraid the pickin's are slim for your midday repast, Miss Hannah," Bolton said as he stepped into view holding a tray in one hand and a folding chair in the other. "I haven't had a chance to make a grocery run lately. So lunch is only a grilled cheese with sliced andouille sausage, Jell-O salad mold, and sweet tea. Please forgive my lapsed hospitality. I hope to remedy the situation before dinnertime."

He looked at her hesitantly, as if he feared he might have offended her. Hannah knew it was all part of his act. Bolton wasn't really worried about her reaction. He just wanted to reinforce the notion that he was more than simply her kidnapper. He was her host, her protector, perhaps even her friend. It was an image he'd cultivated almost from the start of her captivity, at least after she'd given up the screaming.

She wasn't sure what his motivation was. But she was certain he had one and that at some point soon, he would reveal it. She got the distinct impression that he was less interested in killing her than winning her over, which seemed to be an odd goal for a murdering kidnapper. But she preferred it to the alternative.

"I propose we try something different today," he said as he placed the tray on the ground in front of her, set up the folding chair, and sat down.

Hannah, who was seated cross-legged on the dirt floor with her back resting against the wooden beam in the center of the room, reached for the tray.

"What's that?" she asked, before taking a huge bite out of the sandwich.

"I was thinking I might unchain you."

Hannah almost choked on her food.

"What?" she managed to garble.

"I think it's time, don't you?"

"I didn't know I had a vote in the matter," she said incredulously.

"Well, not officially. But I consider your input valuable to the decision-making process. Do you think it's a good idea, Miss Hannah?"

"You're asking me if I think you should release me from the chains that have kept me confined to a six-foot area for the last week? I'm going to go with a strong 'yes' on that one, Bolton."

Bolton smiled. He seemed to get a kick out of her using his first name. Maybe he thought it meant she was warming up to him. What he didn't know was that Hannah liked to throw first names back at people like they were an insult. Or maybe he knew and just didn't care.

"There is a condition, of course," he added.

"Of course," she said.

"You have to give your word, on your honor, that you won't run."

Hannah stared at him as if he was crazy, which she suspected he might very well be.

"Now why would I ever do that?" she asked sarcastically.

"I mean it. I will unloose your chains if you promise me you won't try to escape. And to sweeten the pot, I'll make a second offer. If you can prove to me that you are worthy of hearing it, I will share a secret that I think you might find very interesting."

"What kind of secret?" she asked, hating herself for showing any interest at all.

"Your secret, Miss Hannah—I will share *your* secret."

"What the hell does that even mean?" she demanded.

Bolton leaned back in his chair, a frown on his face.

"You know, I would have thought that being snatched from your home and held against your will would have chastened you a bit. But it seems that not even a double murder and kidnapping can prevent a teenager from spewing attitude."

Hannah, realizing she had gotten a little too comfortable, reeled herself back in.

"I'm sorry," she said, trying to sound sincere. "I would very much like for you to unchain me. I promise I won't run."

Bolton broke into a toothy smile.

"Now that's more like it," he said, standing up and walking over.

He pulled out a key and unchained her wrists and ankles. Hannah immediately began rubbing the raw areas. He returned to his seat and waited patiently while she finished her meal. When she was done he nodded to the metal bucket in the corner.

"If things go well," he said, "I might dispense with that contraption and let you use a flushable toilet upstairs."

"Will wonders never cease," she declared dramatically before batting her eyes at him. "You have to give me the occasional outburst, Bolton, or I'll complete lose it down here."

"Fair enough," he agreed, as he stood up to collect her tray. "Just don't make a habit of it. That kind of mockery isn't very ladylike."

Hannah couldn't help but notice that, as he gathered up her things, his back was to her. If she wanted, now was the perfect opportunity to make that run for it she'd assured him she wouldn't try. The stairs were unblocked. The door at the top was open. She might never get a better chance.

But something held her back. It certainly wasn't any promise she'd made. Maybe that meant something in his fevered, chivalry-obsessed mind. But to her they were just words.

More likely, it could have been the fact that she hadn't tried to run, or even walk, more than twenty feet in the last seven days and the likelihood that she could outpace Bolton Crutchfield was remote. It might have been her certainty that somewhere upstairs was at least one, and probably multiple, traps designed to prevent her from going anywhere.

Or it could have been something else, something she wasn't inclined to admit out loud; something she could barely acknowledge to herself. She was intrigued.

She wanted to know that secret.

So she stayed put.

CHAPTER NINE

"Hold on tight," Ryan said as he hung up the phone and hit the accelerator. Jessie clutched the door handle and braced as he banked hard to the left.

"You want to tell me what that call was?" she asked.

"That was Detective Dunlop," he said as he swerved to avoid a garbage truck. "He just got a tip from one of his pawn shop owner contacts. The guy says a woman is in his place at this very moment trying to pawn a Rolex with the initials 'G.M.' inscribed on the back. He's stalling her until we can get there."

Okay," Jessie said, pressing her feet hard into the car floor. "But if you don't slow down when we get closer, she's going to hear your tires screeching and know something's up." He nodded apologetically.

Despite feeling justified in chastising him in the moment, Jessie couldn't shake the larger sense of guilt she felt. Ryan, focused on navigating the busy downtown lunchtime traffic, seemed oblivious to Jessie's internal debate. But even as the car swerved in and out of lanes, she couldn't stifle the feeling that she should be straight with him.

They'd been through a lot together, including multiple life-threatening situations, several hospitalizations, hunts for and escapes from serial killers, not to mention two divorces. And yet she still hadn't felt she could tell him about her secret deal with Garland Moses.

Part of it was to protect him from retaliation if Decker found out. But she had to admit that part of it was to protect herself too. After being burned by her ex, Kyle, and nearly murdered by her own father, she was reluctant to truly open up and share everything with anyone, especially someone she was interested in. After all, that's the kind of person who could hurt her the most.

But didn't he deserve the benefit of the doubt, after all this time? She glanced over at him and felt a wave of gratitude. The last few years had been very rocky for her. They had cost her a husband, her oldest friend, Lacy, and her adoptive parents. But somehow she'd forged new connections. Kat Gentry had become what she imagined a sister must be like. But Ryan had been her rock through all of it, always there, always supportive, always on her side.

Maybe I ought to tell him that.

She resolved to do it, though this wasn't the ideal time. Ryan screeched to a halt just outside the Perfect Pawns storefront and they leapt out. Even from outside, they could see the blonde woman.

She was facing away from them, talking across the counter to the clearly agitated proprietor, who was desperately trying not to stare at them. They slowed to a crisp trot as they entered the store, which caused a gentle beep that made the woman turn around.

She looked at them apprehensively. Jessie gave her a quick once-over. She was attractive. But up close, one could see pock marks on her cheeks that suggested she'd had bad acne when she was younger. She looked harder and colder than the footage at the hotel had suggested. And without the trench coat to leave something to the imagination, her figure wasn't quite as va-va-voomy as Jessie remembered.

"How are you doing, ma'am?" Ryan asked in a tone that wasn't nearly as friendly as he'd intended.

The woman instantly sensed something was wrong. But to her credit, she remained cool, not even glancing down at the watch in her hand as she plastered a forced smile on her face.

"I'm good," she said enthusiastically. "How are you two doing? Looking for an engagement ring maybe? Sal here has some great stuff. If I was getting hitched, I'd come here looking for a good deal."

"It looks like you know quality work when you see it," Jessie said, nodding at the watch. "Are you buying or selling?'

The woman's face twitched slightly at the question; she was well aware that there was no easy answer for someone in her position.

"Always looking," she finally managed, which Jessie thought was a decent effort under the circumstances.

"I see it has an inscription," Jessie replied. "Is it romantic? Do you mind if I take a look? I love romantic quotes."

The blonde woman sighed, seeming to sense there was no way out of this for her. Neither Ryan nor Jessie had yet revealed they were law enforcement but the woman smelled it coming off them.

"You go right ahead," she said, placing it on the counter. "I need to use the ladies' room anyway. You don't mind, do you, Sal?"

Sal had barely opened his mouth to respond before she hopped over the counter and darted toward the back exit. Ryan followed the same way, pulling out his weapon as he chased her down the narrow hall that led to the back alley. Sal lifted the hinged portion of the counter so that Jessie could get by without having to try to leap across and recreate a scene from *The Dukes of Hazzard*.

By the time she pushed open the door to the alley, the action was already over. Ryan had the woman pressed up against a chain-link fence as he hand-cuffed her and began reading her rights. When he was done, he turned around and gave Jessie a wink.

"Nice to get back on the horse," he said.

"Okay, cowboy," Jessie replied, amused at his childlike enthusiasm. He looked like he'd just finished a great game of cops and robbers. "Why don't you put her in the car? I'll go back and get the watch."

She turned around and headed back inside. Just before the door closed, she could have sworn she heard him yell out, "Yeehaw!"

"I didn't steal it!"

It was the third time the blonde woman, whose street name was Cherry and real name was Cherie Frazier, had made the claim.

"You keep saying that," Ryan said as he stared at her across the interrogation room table. "But it was stolen and you had it. What other conclusion are we supposed to draw, Cherie?"

"And I keep telling you, that information is going to cost you. I want a deal if I'm gonna rat someone out."

"Cherie," Ryan said patiently. "Do you really think we care that much? We have you dead to rights for the watch. This isn't a 'make a deal' kind of situation.

It's a 'slam dunk, convicted in ten minutes, throw you in the slammer for two years' case of theft. Unless you give me something more significant than that in the next five seconds, I'm turning our report over to the DA. At that point, it's out of my hands."

He looked through the one-way glass with an exasperated expression on his face. Jessie knew the look was intended for her. He thought this was a waste of time and that they should just go at her directly about the murder.

But Jessie had convinced him to hold off. Something about Cherie didn't sit right with her. She didn't carry herself with the anxiety of someone who thought she was about to be caught for another, larger crime. She was acting like someone who'd been busted for the actual crime she'd committed and was trying to weasel out of it.

That didn't make sense. If she had killed Gordon Maines and she thought she could skate by on a theft conviction, one would have expected her to jump at the chance, not extend the interrogation.

"Listen, man," Cherie insisted. "I'm not going down for something I didn't do. Yeah, I was gonna pawn the watch. But I didn't steal it. I bought it, thinking I got it for a song. If you're so hot to know who I got it from, I might be able to help you out there. But if you want her that bad, you gotta give me immunity."

Jessie's ears perked up. Within seconds she was out of the observation room and opening the door to the interrogation room. She entered just in time to hear a flabbergasted Ryan say, "...not giving you immunity. This isn't a mob movie. We're not taking down Vito Corleone here."

He was about to continue when he caught the look in Jessie's eye and walked over.

"What is it?" he asked.

"Do you trust me?" she countered.

"Does a billy goat wear boxers in the winter?" he asked, smiling.

Jessie's mouth dropped open.

"I have no response to that," she said.

"I trust you," he said. "Go ahead."

Jessie turned her attention to Cherie, who was eyeing her curiously. The other woman spoke first.

"You've got potential," she said, looking Jessie up and down. "I know guys who would definitely go for the athletic Amazon thing you've got going on. If you ever get got tired of saving the world from legitimate watch pawners, I might have a gig for you."

Jessie had been taunted by far worse than the likes of Cherie and moved right past the offer to her own question.

"Did you say you got the watch from a 'her'?" she asked sharply.

Cherie leaned back in her chair, surprised that someone seemed to actually be taking her seriously.

"If I answer that, you gonna give me immunity, Wonder Woman?"

"No. But if you have information that bears out, we might go to the DA and suggest a reduced sentence, maybe even probation. If you're really a legitimate watch pawner, then that should sound like solid offer."

"How do I know I can trust you?" Cherie asked.

Jessie pointed at the camera in the corner of the room.

"You've already been read your rights. Everything we say and do in here is being recorded. So if I screw you over, you'll have the footage at trial. I'm telling you that if you answer all our questions honestly and your information is helpful in another investigation, we will strongly advise the prosecutor's office to take that into account when charging you. I can't guarantee what they'll do. But we usually have influence in this kind of situation. Of course, if it turns out that you're just playing us, we'll recommend they throw the book at you. Deal?"

Cherie looked at her with a jaundiced eye. Jessie doubted the woman had often been in a position to negotiate her way out of trouble. She seemed unsure what to do with her unexpected power. Out of the corner of her eye, Jessie saw Ryan shift his weight and sensed his impatience.

"One-time offer," she prompted.

That helped Cherie make up her mind.

"Deal," she agreed.

"Right," Jessie replied, diving right in before Cherie could change her mind. "Tell me about the woman who sold you the watch. Describe her and how it happened."

"Okay," Cherie said, leaning back in her chair and scrunching up her face as if that might better retrieve the memory. "I met her in the restroom of the bar at Hotel Figueroa. I was waiting for a ... friend to show up. She walked in. I was freshening up and we got to talking."

"What did you talk about?" Jessie asked.

"Well, I could tell she was in the same line of work and we started swapping war stories. She mentioned that she'd just had a date where the guy paid her with his watch—said it was worth way more than her rate. She took it but now she was worried that her... manager would be pissed that she hadn't demanded cash. She was supposed to meet up with him soon. She looked really anxious about it."

"How so?" Jessie asked.

"She was biting her nails and looked real twitchy, not drug twitchy, scared twitchy."

"So what happened?"

"I looked at the watch. It was legit. I used to sell... you can't charge me for any bad stuff I used to do, right? Not if I tell you about it outright?"

"As long as it's unrelated to this case, we won't," Jessie promised.

"Okay. I used to sell fake Rolexes on Hollywood Boulevard. I worked for a guy who showed me how to spot fakes from the real thing. I could tell this was real. So I offered to buy it off her at a discount. I offered her a grand. I wasn't trying to snow her or anything. She knew it was worth lots more but she needed cash fast. So she said yes. We made the trade. She left. I finished getting cleaned up and went out to the bar to meet my friend."

"You'd never met this woman before?" Jessie asked.

"Not that I remember. And I think I would have."

"Why?" Ryan asked, speaking up for the first time since Jessie had taken over the questioning. "What did she look like?"

Cherie gave him a dirty look, like she still resented his refusal to give her immunity earlier. But she answered anyway.

"She was unbelievable. I'm actually glad we don't travel in the same circles because—I'm willing to admit—I couldn't compete if she was around."

"Why not?" Jessie asked.

"First, she had these amazing, piercing blue eyes. I mean, she could probably hypnotize people with them. I could have stared at her for days. Also, she had this body that looked like something out of the Victoria's Secret catalog. And she wasn't just pretty. She was... what's the right word? Stunning! I mean, the girl shouldn't have been working the bars. She should have been in the valley getting paid to work it on camera. You know what I mean?"

"I do," Jessie said, trying to sound like she was down with the San Fernando Valley porn scene. "What else can you tell us about her?"

"She had medium-length black hair," Cherie said, making Jessie glance over at Ryan.

"Are you sure?" she asked. Their suspect was blonde.

"Yeah, of course. She said she was considering dyeing it blonde but that her hairdresser said it would look fake since hers was so dark."

"Wig?" Ryan mouthed questioningly, suspecting the same thing as Jessie— that the blonde hair they'd seen in the surveillance footage might have been part of the killer's disguise.

"What else?" Jessie asked, choosing not to linger on that detail for now. "Did you notice anything unusual? Any tattoos? Scars? Did she have an accent?"

"No accent that I could tell," Cherie said. "She sounded normal."

"Normal?" Ryan asked.

"Like she was from here, not Alabama or New York or something."

"Ah yes, normal," Ryan said drily.

"Anything else?" Jessie asked.

"No tattoos that I could see. She did have a mark on her left shoulder, kind of angry looking."

"What kind of mark?" Jessie pressed.

"I would say it looked like one of those vaccination scars that older people have."

"Like a smallpox vaccination scar?" Ryan asked.

"I guess. But she's too young for that. It could have been a burn or something. It was about the size of a nickel. It looked like she'd put some makeup on it earlier but it had mostly worn off."

"What else?" Jessie asked.

"That's it. She was pretty normal other than being super-hot and trying to sell the watch on the cheap."

Before they could continue, there was a knock on the door and Camille Guadino, the rookie tech, poked her head in.

"We got the location data back on our victim. I can give you his movements for the hours leading up to the incident. Want to take a look back in our office?"

Jessie looked at Ryan, who nodded yes.

"We'll be there in a minute," he told her.

Jessie turned back to Cherie.

"This is a good start," she said. "We're going to check it out. If we can verify what you've told us so far, we may be in business. I'll probably have a few more questions for you. But sit tight for now, okay?"

"Can I get an ice cream sandwich while I wait?" Cherie asked.

Jessie raised her eyebrows at Ryan.

"We don't have that here," he said. "But someone can get you chips or a granola bar; maybe some coffee."

"That's lame," she protested. "What kind of café do you have here?"

Ryan's face turned red.

"This is a police station, not a restaurant," he snapped.

"We'll see what we can do," Jessie interrupted. "Hang tight. Let's talk outside, Detective."

Once in the hall, she watched Ryan visibly exhale.

"She really gets under your skin, huh?" she said.

"I don't know how she gets people to pay for private time with her," he muttered. "I can barely stand to talk to her."

"I'm not sure her clients care about the latter as long as they get the former. Let's just have someone bring her a collection of snacks. She can take her pick. More importantly, how do we want to work this?"

"Well," Ryan replied, "if she's not our suspect and she's being straight with us, it sounds like the killer isn't a wronged mistress so much as a wronged hooker."

"I think she is being honest," Jessie said. "I had my doubts that she was our gal from the start."

"Why is that?"

"The woman walking down that hotel hallway after she left Maines's room had a poise I just don't see in Cherie. She was so . . . unruffled. She didn't look like she just killed someone so much as that she'd just dropped off her dry cleaning."

"Cherie definitely doesn't give off the unruffled vibe," he agreed.

"No. And she's so scattered. This crime was organized. She had it all planned out. I'm not sure Cherie could plan her next meal. To be honest, I think selling the watch was part of the killer's plan. She must have known she couldn't pawn it herself. And she knew we'd be looking in shops today to see if she'd try. So she got what she could for it and sent us on a wild goose chase, giving it to a woman who looked enough like her that we'd go down a dead end after the lead. I also think she probably got a kick out of selling Gordon's prized watch to a hooker for next to nothing. It feels like adding insult to injury."

"To do that, sell that watch right after offing a guy like it was no big deal, she has to have ice in her veins."

"That's what I'm afraid of," Jessie said.

CHAPTER TEN

They stood quietly in the center of the hall as officers hurried past. Neither of them spoke for a while. They didn't need to. Jessie knew they were both pondering the same thing—the possibility that they might be dealing with something far more sinister than a simple "hooker kills and robs a john" scenario.

Ryan finally broke the silence.

"All of what you said makes sense," Ryan said. "But I don't get something. Why would she spend any time with this Cherie, knowing we would probably find and interview her? She had to know Cherie could describe her."

"That's a great question," she noted. "In fact, it's the one that's eating at me right now. I feel like this woman is manipulating us, like she's one step ahead."

"Maybe the call girl thing is part of that. You think she could be faking that too?"

"I'm not sure," Jessie said, feeling as unsettled as she sounded. "I was hoping to talk to Cherie some more to see if she could help me on that front."

"That sounds good. While you do that, I can look at the data Camille collected and go back over Maines's last few hours. Maybe something will pop."

As he headed off to the tech unit to talk to Camille, Jessie returned to her desk. Before she continued her interrogation of Cherie, she wanted to see if she could confirm what the woman had told her so far.

It didn't take long. Hotel Figueroa was cooperative and sent over their footage from the night before. Within minutes she found verification of Cherie's story. She was sitting in the Bar Figueroa from 10:11 to 10:53, sipping a drink, which officially ruled her out as the potential killer.

At 10:53 she got up and cameras showed her heading in the direction of the ladies' room. Coverage was spotty in that area so she couldn't see anyone actually enter or exit the bathroom. But Cherie did return to the bar at 11:07 p.m., where she joined a man in a navy suit. They left ten minutes later, with his hand on her backside.

Jessie scrolled through the footage a little longer, hoping to catch a glimpse of anyone matching the woman Cherie had described. But there was nothing. She wasn't shocked. If selling the watch was part of her plan, it would have been surprising if she wasn't meticulous about the details of that transaction. She'd avoided every camera at the Bonaventure. Doing the same at Hotel Figueroa just made sense. But the timing fit. The hotels were on the same street, only minutes apart. Maines's killer could have easily hopped a ride share or cab and made it to the second hotel by 10:55.

Jessie returned to the interrogation room to talk to Cherie. Now that she knew her witness was generally telling the truth, she hoped to learn some more about how her world worked. Maybe if she knew how one call girl in downtown L.A. operated, she could get some insight into another.

It wasn't like Jessie had never been exposed to the world of prostitution. In fact, she had a very personal connection. But her experience was limited to the wealthy enclaves of Orange County.

It turned out that her ex-husband's mistress—the one he'd murdered and tried to frame Jessie for killing—was actually part of a prostitution ring secretly run out of the yacht club where the couple had been members. Despite that unpleasant association, it didn't help her much here. The world of L.A. prostitution was unfamiliar to her.

She returned to the interrogation room, where she found Cherie happily alternating between Twinkie bites and Snapple sips.

"It looks like your info is panning out so far," Jessie told her as she sat down across the table from her. "If you keep up the good work, we may have a deal. But I have some more questions for you."

"Brnng oot," Cherie muttered with a full mouth.

Assuming she was saying "bring it," Jessie considered how best to do that. She needed to be delicate in her approach to the next question. Finally she dipped a conversational toe in the water.

"You said you could tell the woman in the bathroom was in the same line of work as you. How could you be so sure?"

What Jessie didn't say was that she wasn't a hundred percent sure the killer was a call girl. Cherie had a hard, beaten-down look. Though only twenty-four according to her rap sheet, she had the appearance of someone a decade older, who'd been in this life for quite a while. The killer projected none of that. Despite her apparent crime, the woman in that hotel footage looked somehow . . . softer.

It was clear that she could turn on the seductive charm at will. And physically, she did not project innocence by any stretch. But she didn't look worn down by the world. She had a vibrancy to her that suggested her spirit hadn't yet been crushed. Jessie wondered just how much hooking experience she actually had, if any. She seemed like a comparative newbie.

"She knew the lingo," Cherie answered, unoffended. "She was up on the right hotels to go to. But it was more than that. She had the 'eyes in the back of the head' thing."

"What's that?" Jessie asked.

"It's a thing working girls have. You never know what kind of guy you're dealing with. Even if it's a regular, there's always the chance that he might get rough. So your head is always on a swivel whenever you're working—in bed, in a bar, on the street, even in a restroom. No matter how comfortable you are, you can't get too comfortable—eyes in the back of your head."

"And she had it?" Jessie reconfirmed.

"She oozed it."

Hours later, Jessie was still poring over footage from both Hotel Figueroa and the Bonaventure in a vain attempt to catch sight of Blue Eyes, as she'd mentally begun referring to their unnamed killer.

With an assurance from Cherie that she'd answer any future questions, Jessie had left the wrangling over a plea and reduced sentence to her court-appointed lawyer and the lowly prosecutor assigned to the case.

Somewhere in the middle of parsing the footage, she'd also gotten a crash course in the world of modern prostitution from Detective Gaylene Parker of the Vice unit. The tutorial had been overwhelming. Apparently the "money for sex" system had changed dramatically in recent years.

No longer did women just post ads in the back of alternative weeklies or on bare-bones websites. Now the whole operation involved apps, online aliases, and dummy social media accounts. Some men even had memberships in exclusive "clubs" that required entry fees and background checks.

Jessie had dealt with a case last year that involved something similar—an online club for prospective cheating husbands. But that was a mom-and-pop operation compared to the magnitude of this business. When she finally accepted the realization that understanding the minutiae of the whole thing would take days, not hours, she resignedly returned to the comparatively satisfying task of looking at grainy hotel videos. It was only when Ryan tapped her on the shoulder that she realized how long she'd been staring at screens.

"What time is it?" she asked.

"Almost nine p.m.," he answered.

"It's dark out," Jessie noted, looking out the window. "When did that happen?"

"Well, Jessie," he said, sitting down across from her, "it happened over the course of several hours. You see, as it gets later in the day, the sun begins to set..."

"Shut up, smart-ass," she said, unable to hide her smile. "Why didn't you come by earlier?"

"I did actually," he said. "But you were so immersed in studying that footage that I didn't want to break your concentration. Besides, I was having some fun of my own looking at location data from Gordon Maines's phone."

"Find anything good?"

"We were able to pinpoint his movements for the entire day. None of it is unusual. Lots of meetings, constituent calls, fundraising events—that kind of stuff. It's only later in the evening that things get interesting."

"How so?" Jessie asked, finally tearing her eyes away from her screen.

"It looks like Maines's phone auto-connected to the Gallery Bar at the Millennium Biltmore Hotel around nine fifteen last night."

"Why is that significant?"

"Well, do you remember how it looked like Maines knew the killer—or had at least met her before—when she walked up to him at the Lobby Court bar at the Bonaventure?"

"Yeah. By the way, we're calling her Blue Eyes now."

"Okay," Ryan said, not missing a beat. "I'm wondering if maybe Maines and Blue Eyes met at the Biltmore first and then she instructed him to reconnect with her at the Lobby Court bar later. That way she could determine if he was serious. Plus she could see if he was alone, maybe tail him to see if he was a Vice cop."

"That's not a crazy hypothesis, Ryan," Jessie said, thinking about Cherie's "eyes in the back of the head" theory. "You may have a future in this business after all."

"Thanks." He rolled his eyes.

Jessie looked at the clock. Suddenly she stood straight up.

"It's eight fifty-eight," she said, only now registering the significance of the time that Ryan had mentioned earlier. "That's almost when Maines went to the Gallery Bar at the Biltmore last night. It makes me wonder—what if she uses that bar regularly to scout potential johns before sending them elsewhere to hook up? If that's the case, she might be there right now. You interested in checking out a local watering hole?"

"You read my mind," Ryan replied, grabbing his jacket. "Let's go."

"Just one second," Jessie said as she printed out the clearest screen grab she had of Blue Eyes. "It's not much. But maybe this will help."

Ryan nodded, but she could tell from his expression that he doubted the image would be enough to ID Blue Byes. Unfortunately, she agreed.

CHAPTER ELEVEN

Alex Cutter sat at the hotel bar. As she sipped her martini, she used the bar mirror to keep an eye on anyone who came within touching distance of her. She was used to being grabbed, pinched, rubbed, and worse. But she was less likely to flinch if she saw it coming.

She'd been nursing the drink for a solid half hour, since 8:30, while she looked for potential prospects. Two guys had already approached her but she'd politely given both the brush-off. The first didn't look like he could afford her. The second, while clearly well off, had a sad, schlubby vibe that just wouldn't do.

She needed a candidate who met all her requirements. He had to be rich, for sure. He had to have a position of power in his profession. He had to have the confidence—arrogance maybe—to think he was good-looking enough to get her without paying for it. Mostly though, he had to be an asshole.

For a moment, she wondered if she was sending out the wrong signals and gave herself a once-over in the bar mirror. Everything seemed to be working. The long, straight black hair shimmied down her back, tickling her exposed skin. The slit of her yellow skirt ran tantalizingly, though not vulgarly, high. Her makeup was impeccable. Then she noticed it. She wasn't smiling.

In order to draw in the biggest fish, the smile was the bait. Not an open, warm friendly smile. Instead, the kind of man she wanted to lure in was looking for the "I've got a secret and I'm willing to share it with the right guy" smile. She'd been so focused on the big goal that she'd neglected that one little thing. But it was always the little things that made the biggest difference. She licked her lips and let them relax.

That's better.

She settled in, confident that her prey would arrive soon. It was just a matter of time now.

As she pretended to study her drink, and with her eyes still on high alert, Alex allowed her thoughts to drift slightly. It was only a few months ago that she'd been living a far different life. The folks back home in Vegas would barely recognize her now.

Alex ran a finger along the carefully covered, coin-sized scar on her left shoulder, the one her stepfather had given her when she was fifteen.

One day, while driving her home from school, he stopped behind an abandoned warehouse to "get to know her a bit better." She had refused and struggled, accidentally nailing him in the nose with a flailing elbow. He didn't like that very much.

His truck had one of those old, push-in cigarette lighters, which he used to let her know how he felt. Then he asked if she planned to get uppity anymore. Through her sobs, Alex said no. She didn't fight after that when he got to know her better. Not that day. Not for the next two years.

But when he brought over some buddies to meet her one night when her mom was working the overnight shift at the diner, she reached her breaking point. They tried to hold her down in the living room but she managed to wriggle free and get to her bedroom.

She locked the door, threw her coat, phone, and the $268 she'd been saving into a backpack, grabbed the bread knife she kept under her mattress, and started for the window. That's when her stepfather kicked down the door. With his friends egging him on, he ran toward her.

It was dark and he was moving fast, so he didn't see the knife she was clutching and ran right into it. She let go as he tumbled back onto the floor. She heard his friends stop cheering but was out the window before the real yelling started. She heard her dog, Lola, barking in the distance as she ran down the street. It took all her willpower not to go back for the only living creature that truly seemed to love her unconditionally.

After that, things got rough for a while. She bought some wigs and heavy makeup from a showgirl supply shop so she could disguise herself in case the cops came looking for her. But they never did and she didn't see any stories on the news. She suspected it might be hard for her stepfather to credibly explain how he was stabbed so he likely didn't call the authorities.

Still, she didn't dare try to stay with any of her friends, or with the guy she'd been dating, mostly because he was nice (he didn't talk dirty when they did it). The chances of someone calling her mom were too great. So she he stayed in crappy motels in the Fremont Street district until most of her cash ran out, which took about a week.

After that, she had to make some hard decisions. She tried to get work at one of the local strip clubs but the minimum age was eighteen and she was still a few months shy. A manager at one of the clubs said to come back on her birthday. In the meantime, he gave her the number of a friend who could get her temporary work.

Alex wasn't surprised when the work involved dressing up in a Catholic schoolgirl uniform and, along with other girls, performing at a bachelor party. After that, it became a regular thing. It was a cash business and no ID or W-2 was required. The money was okay, enough to get her a room in a weekly hotel with a shared bathroom for twelve people and a futon for a bed.

Once she learned that a few of the other girls who did extra stuff on the side at the parties pulled in about $300 to $500 more a night than she did, it wasn't a huge leap to join them. She was already more than used to letting older guys do what they wanted to her while she mentally tuned out. Getting paid for it seemed like a fair trade. And because her physical proportions dovetailed with these guys' fantasies, she got well compensated.

From there, it didn't take long for her to set up private dates. That money was even better. And now that she was eighteen and could work the strip clubs too, she had more control over her private clientele.

But eventually she got tired of having to split half her take with the house. Even the security they provided for privates didn't seem like it was worth it, especially since usually by the time they showed up to deal with a problem, the john had gotten in his fair share of licks. Those licks meant bruises, which made it hard to get new johns. After all, who would want to get with a girl who was black and blue all over, unless he was the one who'd done it?

So she went the independent route and decided to become her own security detail. She took karate three days a week and had just gotten her brown belt when it happened. She should have known better when he insisted on having the date at his place instead of her preferred motel, the one where she could deadbolt the bathroom door and squeeze through the bars over the shower window if necessary.

But he was cute and well-dressed and smelled clean. Plus he gave her $100 up front, one third of her standard fee. So she went back to his place, a house in Henderson that was twenty minutes southeast of the city. She figured she could take a Lyft back.

Everything was standard for a while. The guy, Dan, wanted her to tie him up. She did, using pillowcases, but loose enough that he could break free if he got skittish. A lot of guys got skittish. Then Dan had her get into a naughty maid costume and clean up his bedroom. Eventually he told her to clean *him* up. It was all going well. In fact, it was borderline boring. Maybe that's why she let her guard down.

Dan was lying on his back in bed and she was sucking on one of his toes, as he'd requested. So she didn't see him pull out the baseball bat. By the time she caught a glimpse of him swinging it toward her, she barely had time to throw up her arms and block the blow.

The force knocked her backward and she tumbled off the bed. Her forearms were throbbing as she tried to orient herself. Dan got out of the bed and came at her fast, swinging again. This time she managed to get only one hand up, enough to just slightly diminish the force of the bat before it slammed into the left side of her ribcage.

She toppled over. Her side was screaming, though she couldn't make a sound because the wind had been knocked out of her. Dan lifted the bat again, but apparently seeing her diminished state, felt another whack was unnecessary. So he tossed it aside, leaned down, grabbed Alex by the hair, and dragged her over to the bed.

He threw her against the headboard, stunning her. She was still dazed, slipping in and out of consciousness, when she realized that he'd tied her wrists to the bed, only he hadn't done it loosely. She felt the circulation beginning to cut off in her fingers as he ripped off what remained of the maid uniform.

He climbed on top of her and began to do his thing. The weight of his body against hers was excruciating, especially when he pressed against her ribs, which she suspected were broken. He slapped her a few times but compared to the pain in her arms and torso, that was more of a nuisance.

After he was done, he rolled off her and went to the bathroom. It was only when she heard the faucet running that she began yanking at the pillowcases he'd used to tie her wrists to the bed posts. It took several minutes of tugging before the right hand eventually came loose. With her fingers still numb, she desperately tried to untie the other one. It finally came free as she heard the faucet being turned off.

She scrambled off the bed as she heard the door open. The bat was lying on the ground where he'd tossed it. She picked it up, squeezing tight for fear her still-numb fingers might not maintain their grip.

When he rounded the corner to the bed, she swung. Though it wasn't with as much force as she would have liked, the swing hit its target, slamming directly into Dan's forehead. He looked more stunned than injured as he stumbled backward, slamming into his dresser.

His back bent unnaturally backward in the collision and she could tell he'd tweaked something. He bent over, seemingly uncertain whether to attend to that or his head. As he stood up straight again, Alex advanced, rearing the bat back and rocking it forward. Dan was just looking up when the barrel hit his left temple.

He stood upright a second longer, like a just-sawed tree in the moment before it topples over. Then he crumpled to the ground. Until then then he'd been too stunned to speak. But now a loud sound—a mix of groan and scream—escaped his lips. He tried to reach his hand up to his bleeding head but was disoriented and had trouble finding it.

Alex stepped toward him and reared back again. Dan seemed to sense the threat and threw his hands up to cover his head. But she had anticipated that. This time she swung from below, like the bat was a golf club. She came up hard and fast, connecting with the bottom of Dan's chin. His mouth snapped shut and the screaming stopped.

He slumped backward and his head slammed on the floor. He appeared to be unconscious. But Alex didn't care. She swung, this time landing a blow on his face and crushing his left cheekbone. She swung at the head again. And again. And another time after that.

She lost count of how many times she smashed the barrel of the bat into Dan's head. But by the time her arms finally gave out and the bat slipped from her shaking fingers, he was unrecognizable. His skull looked like a watermelon that had been cracked into multiple pulpy chunks.

Alex sat down on the bed and allowed herself to breathe. She felt the adrenaline course through her system. Every part of her tingled. The pain in her head and ribs and forearms and wrists and fingers seemed distant. She felt her body give up and didn't fight it as she collapsed onto the bed. She just needed a second to regroup. When she woke up, it was morning.

Cleaning up was easier than Alex expected.

For some reason, when her eyes opened that next morning, she felt refreshed and invigorated. Yes, she hurt all over. But some part of her was able to compartmentalize the physical pain so she could accomplish the tasks at hand.

She reminded herself that she had time. The date had been on a Friday night. As she glanced over at Dan's broken visage, she remembered that he had told her he worked for a corporate bank. So he wouldn't be expected into the office until Monday.

She stayed naked as she moved around, so that she wouldn't get her clothes soiled. After she dragged his body to the laundry room, she wiped it down with Clorox, especially areas that had interacted with her body. Then she stuffed him into the washing machine. She had to slam the door to get him in completely.

After that, she wiped up the blood-and-brain-covered hardwood bedroom floor. Next, she put on a pair of his gloves and bleached and wiped down every surface she'd touched. She took the sheets, pillowcases, and maid outfit and tossed them in his fireplace. After showering and bleaching the stall, she threw the towel in the fireplace as well.

While the linens and clothes burned, she got dressed and put the bat in a plastic trash bag and then into a duffel bag. She did one last check of the house before locking and leaving it. She tossed the gloves in the duffel bag along with Dan's wallet and walked a mile to the main road, where she caught a bus back to town. Once there, she dumped the trash bag with the bat in a dumpster, the gloves in another one six blocks over, and the duffel bag in a third a quarter mile in the other direction.

Only then did she walk home, where she took a second shower and slept the rest of the day. When she woke up, the sun was setting. She went up onto the roof and sat there, watching the bright reds and oranges on the desert horizon fade into pinks, purples, blues, and finally darkness. For the first time in over three years, she felt free, like a weight she didn't even know she'd been carrying had been lifted off her. It was magical.

Back in the District on the Bloc bar at the Sheraton Grand Hotel in downtown Los Angeles, Alex felt a tap on her shoulder. She looked over to see who she'd reeled in.

"I know you," the man said.

For a second she thought she'd been made and that this was a cop telling her she was busted.

But after only an extra moment's glance, she understood that was not what he meant at all. By saying "I know you," he really just meant "I know what you are, what you're doing here." It was a perfunctory, unimaginative proposal.

But to Alex, that was actually a selling point.

He'll do just fine.

CHAPTER TWELVE

At that time of night, the drive from the police station to the Biltmore Hotel only took four minutes. But that was long enough for the shame to hit Jessie.

It was only as she sat in the passenger's seat of the car that she realized she'd completely forgotten about Hannah. She'd been so immersed in the details of this case, so happy to be back on the hunt, that her half-sister's predicament didn't enter her mind for hours.

She was tempted to call Garland Moses right now, but she managed to fight the urge. Apart from the fact that Ryan, who knew nothing about the old profiler's involvement, would hear everything, she once again reminded herself that Garland would have surely contacted her if he had news. Besides, she didn't want to piss the guy off. It was quite possible that the man was already in bed, settling in with a glass of warm milk or iced scotch. She had to leave it be.

The issue became moot when Ryan pulled up into the loading zone in front of the Biltmore. He flashed his badge at the valet who was about to object as they ran inside. They sprinted up the stairs from the lower lobby into the long hallway that ran the length of the hotel. Directly across from them was the entrance to the Gallery Bar. Only then did the two of them slow down to a brisk walk. Ryan turned to Jessie.

"You take the back and I'll check things out up here," he said. "Let me know discreetly if you see any potential candidates."

Jessie nodded and walked to the back of the bar, putting on her best "I'm here for a chill time" persona as she wandered around, passing large couches and cozy nooks along the walls. Out of the corner of her eye, she saw Ryan move among the tables up front with an equal level of practiced casualness.

As she walked, Jessie let her eyes fall on every blonde in the room. At that hour, there were a lot. But even in the bar's dim light, it was clear that none of them, not even the ones who looked like they too might be working tonight, came even close to approximating Blue Eyes. When she met Ryan in the middle of the bar, she could tell from his expression that he'd had no luck either.

"You want to check out the ladies' room, just in case?" he asked.

Jessie did so, going down the long hallway next to the bar, past the photos on the walls showing the ballroom where several 1930s Oscar ceremonies had been held, and walked into the massive restroom. Jessie actually knew this hotel well and used to love to wander its ornate, old Hollywood halls for fun. But there was no time for that now.

She loitered in the ladies' room for a few minutes until it was empty so she could peek under the stall doors to make sure no one was inside. When she returned to the bar, she caught Ryan's eye and shook her head.

"Let's check with the bartender," she suggested when they reconvened.

Despite the crowd, Jessie was quickly able to get his attention.

"What can I get you, darlin'?" he asked, ignoring Ryan completely.

Jessie was slightly embarrassed to discover she liked the annoyed look she saw on the detective's face. She sensed it wasn't about the drinks as much as the familiarity of the barkeep. She didn't let on that the guy, while good-looking in an overly tanned, highlighted hair kind of way, wasn't her type.

"Seltzer, please," she said sweetly before cutting to the chase. "Were you working around this time last night?"

He looked at her, mildly surprised.

"I'm guessing you don't come in here often, darling, or you'd know I'm here almost every night from eight to one. I promise I'd remember you."

"That's sweet," she replied, batting her eyes, enjoying this playful moment and the effect it was having on Ryan before she went in for the kill. "After you get that seltzer, I'm going to need you to have someone cover the bar for a few minutes. I have a few questions for you. What's your name?"

"The name's Brad. And this isn't usually how it works, you know," he said, still not totally getting it. "Usually we flirt *while* I work the bar. Then we hang out privately afterward."

Jessie smiled, marveling at both his cluelessness and his Neanderthal flattery.

"We're going to need that private hangout now, Brad," she said, leaning in conspiratorially. "Just you, me, and my friend here. His name is Detective Ryan Hernandez of the LAPD."

She watched Brad's face fall and almost felt bad for him. Almost.

"Give me a minute," he muttered as he skulked off.

"You're mean," Ryan said to her, though he was grinning.

"Was that mean?" she asked innocently. "I was just being cordial."

A few minutes later, they were sitting at a corner table with Brad, who looked especially pouty. Jessie showed him the photo, which he dismissed with just a passing glance.

"Don't know her," he said gruffly.

"Brad," Ryan said, speaking for the first time as he leaned back, making sure his jacket fell open to reveal his sidearm, "we're going to need you to do better than that. We're not Vice and we're not interested in any side money you get from girls you might tip off to potential tricks. I'm a homicide detective. That means murder. And you don't want to be uncooperative with a murder investigation."

Brad scowled at him but looked at the photo again anyway.

"Actually, now that I look at it closer, I do recognize her. But I don't know her."

"You don't have a side deal with her to filter guys her way?" Ryan pressed.

"Look, man. I'm not going to say that never happens. But I've never done it with her. She's only been in the bar the one time. I don't even know her name. I've never talked to her other than to take her drink order."

"Are you sure about that?" Jessie challenged him.

"Yes. I wish we did have a deal. She's smokin' hot. And have you seen those eyes? They'd garner an extra Benjamin all on their own. For a while, I actually thought she was some famous actress I didn't recognize. That is, until I saw she was on the job. To be honest, if I didn't worry that she was diseased, I'd take a run at her myself."

Jessie tended to believe Brad's story. It was hard to imagine that a self-involved guy like him would make such distasteful admissions about himself unless he either didn't realize how scummy they made him look, or he was a masterful manipulator. As far as she could tell, Brad wasn't the latter.

"What about this guy?" she asked, showing him the photo of Gordon Maines from his bio on the city website. She was careful to enlarge it so that his name and title weren't visible.

"Yeah, I recognize that guy. He's around a fair bit. I think his name is Gordo. He likes to keep it on the down low but I know he's spent time with a few girls, just never any who commission me."

"Did you see them together last night?"

"It was pretty busy last night," he hedged. "But yeah, I think they were sitting together for a while."

"Why the uncertainty?" Ryan asked.

"I was just trying to be sure because they didn't leave together and I know they paid separate bills. But yeah, they talked for a while."

"Do you remember how they paid?" Jessie asked.

"He used a corporate card. She paid in cash. The girls always pay in cash. Less traceable if they get rounded up, you know?"

Jessie nodded like that detail was common knowledge.

"Did you see her talking to other girls, maybe one that's here now? Did she seem to have any friends?"

"No. There were two things I noticed about that chick above all else. She was a knockout. It was obvious that none of the other girls wanted her around because they paled in comparison. But the other thing was she didn't give off a friendly vibe."

"What kind of vibe did she have?" Jessie asked.

"Focused—like she was on a mission and no one better get in her way. She's a real killer, that one."

CHAPTER THIRTEEN

Devin Schumacher tried to act cool.

He'd been with hookers before. And as a Hollywood agent, he'd been around many attractive women. But something about this girl made him nervous, like a teenager about to lose his virginity. He didn't think he'd ever encountered a woman who was so breathtakingly beautiful but who also just oozed sex. It was a hard combination to pull off but Lexi, as she called herself, somehow managed it.

He sat on the bed of the hotel room in just his boxers and dress shirt, waiting for her to come out of the bathroom. He was a little self-conscious, partly because of his fast-thinning brown hair, partly because of his bony, currently very exposed frame. He took another sip of his cognac, trying to calm his nerves. If his buddies at the agency could see him now, they'd be laughing at him mercilessly.

That was their thing. All the guys in his circle at Artists International— A.I. for short—liked to have a little fun with a professional now and then. Sometimes too much fun, he secretly admitted. But the thing was, these girls would do things their wives and girlfriends wouldn't even consider. As he'd told his boss at a bachelor party just last week, a man had needs, even in this modern era of equality and blah blah blah. That got a good belly laugh.

Devin wasn't married but he was engaged. And truth be told, since they'd started planning the wedding, Debbie had turned into a real ball buster. If her dad wasn't the head of production at a major studio, he'd be reconsidering the whole damn thing.

As it was, he had to content himself with nailing aspiring actresses desperate for representation he'd never provide. And occasionally, as in this case, he gifted himself the skills of the amazing creature that was prepping in the bathroom, the hottest piece of tail he'd seen in years, on camera or off.

Lexi opened the door and stepped out. She was so sexy she seemed almost gauzy, like she had her own lighting crew that was creating a haze around her. She was wearing a slinky, creamy, satin negligee that looked like it might fall off her at any second. Devin blinked a few times, trying to get the visual crispness back. But it wasn't working. The cloudiness in his vision wouldn't go away. It was a serious bummer.

He stood up to approach her but, after a solid first step, he stumbled on the second and careened into the wall, knocking over a picture frame, which shattered loudly on the ground.

He saw Lexi grimace. But she didn't get pissed. Instead she swooped over and wrapped his arm over her shoulder, easing him back toward the bed. He thought he heard her murmur something under her breath but didn't quite catch it.

"Dammit," he muttered. "Don't worry. I'll pay for that."

"It's okay, sweetie," she whispered as she helped him lie down on his back. "I'm sure they've got dozens of those. Don't even worry about it."

"You're so nice," he said, looking up at her as she smiled down at him. "Not like my bitch fiancée. She's a bitch."

"You must really have it rough," she said sympathetically as she pulled his shorts off.

"I really do," he said, noticing that he was slurring his words slightly. "She's always saying, 'let's do this' or 'can we do that?' It's like, shut up, already. Maybe work out for once to get rid of that extra roll instead of spending all your time looking at china patterns, right?"

"Right," Lexi agreed, smiling so broadly that he thought she might be selling something. He watched as she slid on a pair of latex gloves.

"You get it," he said, suddenly worn down by the effort of explaining himself.

"I do," she said, lifting up his right arm and letting it go. It dropped like a log.

"Thaz funneee..." he slurred.

It was like he'd lost complete control of his own body. It felt very heavy and distant, as if it belonged to someone else. He tried to lift his head but found the task impossible. He started to roll over but was surprised to learn that his limbs and torso were totally unresponsive.

"Whaz happing?" he managed to garble.

His teeth felt like tree stumps pressing against his lips, blocking the words from coming out clearly. His tongue seemed to have grown. He conjured an image of a dead snake filling his entire mouth. Lexi sat down beside him on the bed.

"What's happening?" she repeated in a saccharine voice that set off a bell in his quickly dulling brain. "Here's what's happening, sweetie. In a few minutes, you're not going to ever have to worry about your bitchy fiancée ever again. And while it'll be rough for her at first, she'll be better off once she has some distance from the shame of being engaged to a scumbag found dead and naked in a hotel room."

"Whaa?" Devin managed to grunt as he struggled to move away from her. With the last remnants of his muscle control, he ordered his right arm up. It moved weakly, rising slightly and landing on Lexi's hip. He gave her the most perfunctory of shoves.

Lexi looked down at his hand on her and, without warning, slapped him across the face. He knew it must have been hard though he couldn't feel it at all. She was still smiling but something in her bright blue eyes had changed. Even through the fog of his fading vision, they gleamed with a fiery intensity.

"You should have been a nicer person, Devin," she cooed as she brushed his hand off her. "Now you'll forever be known for how you died. Is your mother alive, Devin? I hope she's alive. If she is, the humiliation of this just might kill her. That's on you, big boy."

Only Devin's eyes and ears were still working, so he couldn't make himself understood as he tried to yell "bitch" at her. It came out more like "icchh."

"Because of your clumsiness with the frame, we're in a bit of a rush, Devin. So we better get to it," Lexi said, oblivious to his efforts to speak as she straddled him and wrapped her hands around his throat. "In a few minutes, you'll be dead from the drugs and that would spoil all the fun. Shall we begin?"

CHAPTER FOURTEEN

Jessie took a final swig of her drink.

She didn't normally go for a Seven & Seven but she needed something fizzy and festive to lighten her bleak mood. Ryan, seated across from her at the tiny Gallery Bar corner table, chugged the last of his beer.

"So what now?" she asked for what had to be the third time.

"For tonight, I think this is it," Ryan said. "We are off duty, after all."

"Okay, but what about tomorrow? I think we should set up surveillance at every bar she's hit. Maybe she'll return."

"You really think so?" he asked skeptically. "After what she did, you'd think she want to keep a low profile, maybe lie low for a while, at least work a different part of town."

"Maybe," Jessie said, though she didn't buy it.

"What?" Ryan pressed, sensing her doubt.

"This woman just doesn't strike me as the 'lie low' type. Yeah, she knows when to keep a low profile. But what she did was big and bold. I feel like she's got a taste for it now. I wouldn't be surprised if she tries something similar again."

"You sound almost certain," Ryan noted.

"I kind of am," she admitted, not happily. "I'm actually getting tired of guessing right about the motives and machinations of killers."

"That's sort of your job, Jessie," he said, not meaning to be unkind, but still hitting her where it hurt.

"Not always," she said quietly, her mind drifting to the case she had no professional control over.

"Are you talking about Hannah's abduction?" he asked gently.

She nodded.

"Do you want to talk about it?" he asked. "We've been carefully avoiding it all day."

"I'm not sure I can. Every time I think of her at the mercy of Bolton Crutchfield, I feel my skin crawl. And you want to know the worst part?"

"What?"

"It would be one thing if I thought he was going to kill her. As awful as that would be, I could at least accept that it was out of my hands. After a week, it would be a virtual certainty. But he clearly doesn't want her dead. He wants her corrupted. He wants to make her in my father's image and in his own. So every second that I don't find her is another second he has to infect her mind. And he knows that. I can almost feel him gloating."

Ryan looked like he wanted to say something reassuring but seemed to sense there were no words that would salve her wound. Instead, he simply reached out and grabbed her hand, squeezing it tenderly. To her surprise, she didn't pull away.

"So what now?" she asked for the fourth time.

For the briefest of seconds, she remembered the jealous look on Ryan's face when Brad hit on her. That thought led to the realization that her apartment, the one where he'd been crashing in the living room as her personal bodyguard, was less than a five-minute drive from here.

He smiled in that half endearing, half-cocky way that made everyone from women to witnesses weak-kneed and opened his mouth to offer a suggestion. But before he could get any words out, both their phones buzzed.

Jessie looked down to see an emergency text. It was short and straightforward.

911 call from Sheraton Grand Hotel at 9:47. Body found—male, naked, possibly strangled.

Jessie looked at the time. It was currently 10:01. That meant the call had only come in fourteen minutes ago. The Sheraton Grand Hotel was just four blocks from here. She looked up at Ryan, who was clearly thinking the same thing.

"Maybe she's still there," he said.

Jessie put her glass down and stood up.

"Let's go."

❧   ❧   ❧

Eight minutes later, they stood in the hotel room, looking at the body.

On the way in they'd instructed the uniformed officers to seal all entrances and exits and distributed images of the Blue Eyes screenshot to everyone. They each did a once around of the lobby area and the bar, which yielded nothing. Ryan instructed one officer to go to the security office and review footage from the last hour looking for anyone even vaguely resembling Blue Eyes anywhere on the premises.

Now they stared at the body of the man the hotel register identified as Devin Schumacher. They had to use the hotel's registration system because Devin, in addition to being completely naked, was found without any ID on him, though he did have his cash and phone. Though they couldn't be certain yet, the finger-like bruises already forming on his neck suggested he'd been strangled too.

They were lucky he'd been found at all tonight. The guest in the room next door had heard a loud crashing sound. But hesitant to check it out herself, she called the front desk to let them know. That set a series of steps in motion.

The clerk at the front desk called the room but got no answer. He waited two minutes and called again. Following procedure, he alerted security. The security chief on duty assigned an officer who was monitoring the pool and spa area to make a courtesy check after he finished his rounds.

The officer did, knocking on Devin Schumacher's door only twelve minutes after the guest next door made her original call. Getting no response, he knocked a second time, and then a third. He called down to his duty chief and asked him to call the room one more time. He heard the unanswered phone ring ten times. Then, with official permission from his supervisor, the officer unlocked the door and walked in. That's when he found Devin Schumacher lying dead and naked on the bed.

He radioed his boss, who called 911 and went upstairs himself after ordering two more officers to join him at the room. They secured the entire floor and made sure no one else came in or out until the authorities arrived less than ten minutes later.

Jessie noted silently that, if not for the crashing sound, clearly a result of the picture frame currently resting on the floor near the wall, they wouldn't have learned about Schumacher's death until tomorrow morning at the earliest.

"So," she said after listening to the hotel security chief's rundown. "Less than fifteen minutes from the frame shattering to your officer entering the room. And less than thirty from the crash until our people arrived. Is that right?"

The security chief nodded. Jessie looked over at Ryan, who was doing his own mental math.

"Assuming the frame falling was part of some kind of struggle, then that means Schumacher was still alive at that point. If that's true, then Blue Eyes had about thirteen minutes to kill him, get dressed, take his stuff, wipe everything down, and get out of the room before the officer arrived. That's pretty quick. She'd have to be a really cool customer to pull that off without leaving any traces."

"You're thinking she might have left more evidence than last time because she was in a rush?" Jessie asked.

"I think there's at least a better shot."

"Maybe," she said. "But I'm not holding my breath."

"Why not?"

"She seems very meticulous," Jessie said. "I'd bet she was cautious from the second she entered the room, making sure to touch as few surfaces as possible. I wouldn't be surprised if she had gloves on the whole time. The fewer things she had to remember to wipe down after the fact, the less chance of forgetting something."

"That makes sense," Ryan agreed.

"Plus," Jessie added, thinking of something else. "If she was careful up front and things went bad, like say the drugging didn't work, she could get out of the room clean without leaving prints behind. If the trick called it in, there'd be little to work with."

"So should we just skip the routine?" someone asked from behind them.

Jessie turned around to find a Crime Scene Unit tech staring at her with a sour expression. She knew he wanted her to feel chastened but she was having none of it.

"No," she said sharply. "You go ahead and do your job anyway. And I'll continue to do mine, which is to try and get in this woman's head. You don't mind, do you?"

The tech frowned but said nothing more, sliding grumpily past her.

"Jessie Hunt—always making friends," Ryan said with a wry smile.

"I've got enough friends already," she muttered.

"Really?" he said incredulously. "You've got, like, two."

"Shut up, Detective," she said, though it was hard to generate the venom she intended.

Nothing like flirting over a dead body.

"So with his wallet gone, what do we know about this guy?" she continued quickly, mildly ashamed of herself.

Ryan managed to stifle his chuckle and looked at his phone, on which he'd been doing a web search.

"It looks like Devin Schumacher is a talent agent with A.I. He represents mostly young actors and actresses in features and occasionally, television. He's thirty-three, originally from Shaker Heights, Ohio. Went to Bowling Green State University. He's engaged to a Deborah Morse."

"Great," Jessie said. "That should be another fun conversation."

"At least they're not married. At least he doesn't have kids."

"You want to take a sip from that half-full glass?" she asked him.

"Just looking for a silver lining," Ryan said before turning back to the scene. "So she's in a rush, so much so that she leaves the cash and phone. But she makes sure to take the wallet. Why only that?"

Jessie was starting to get a feel for this girl and answered quickly.

"Because it's not about the robbery. That's just incidental. As we established, there are easier ways to rob a john that don't require killing him. I think she's sending a message."

"To us?" Ryan asked.

"To the johns," Jessie replied. "She wants identifying them to be challenging. She wants their names out there. And she leaves them naked, vulnerable. She wants them shamed, both as they're dying and forever afterward. This is personal. This is payback."

"Like payback against these two guys?" Ryan pressed.

"No. I think it's payback against *all* guys."

CHAPTER FIFTEEN

Hannah woke up with a start.

She could have sworn she heard something. But, other than the sound of the settling house, there was silence in the basement. She glanced up at the small window in the corner and saw total darkness, indicating that it was the middle of the night. Even the neon strip club sign that glowed in the distance had been turned off.

She slowly sat up, trying to orient herself. She felt groggier than usual and wondered if Bolton had slipped some kind of sleeping pill in her dinner. Considering how much leeway he'd given her in the last day, it would have been a surprise. Had something happened to make him feel he had to drug her?

The question made her apprehensive. If he'd drugged her, that meant something had changed, and most of the changes she'd dealt with in the last week had been bad. Was this a sign that he'd grown tired of her and just wanted to keep her sedated until he got rid of her?

But why? In the last day, he'd let her go upstairs to use a real restroom; he'd allowed her to take a shower. He'd put obvious effort into all of her meals. He'd spent hours asking her questions about her life and seemed genuinely interested in the answers.

But now, for reasons she couldn't comprehend, he'd felt the need to change the dynamic. It was almost certainly a sign that time was running out for her. Maybe that meant it was time to do the thing she'd increasingly talked herself out of in recent days: try to escape.

If Bolton thought she was out cold, he might be more lax in his security measures. This might be her best opportunity to get out before... whatever he had planned next.

Hannah scrambled from a seated position to her knees, allowing a second for the subsequent head rush to subside. She was preparing to get to her feet and see if she'd missed some flaw in her captor's plan when she heard something. It was so quiet that she thought she might have imagined it. But then she heard it again. This time she was able to identify it. The sound was a sigh.

"Who's there?" she demanded.

There was no response. But a second later she heard a click and a light came on. The sudden brightness was blinding and she covered her eyes until they could adjust.

"Sorry for the drama, Miss Hannah," a familiar voice said.

When she could see clearly, she looked in his direction and saw Bolton Crutchfield sitting on a folding chair in front of the stairs. It took her a moment to realize he wasn't alone.

Sitting beside him in a heavier wooden chair was another man. He was unconscious and had blood streaming down his forehead from an open wound near his hairline. His glasses were broken and his pudgy face was chalky white. His polo shirt was untucked and a bit of his plump stomach flesh poured out over his tan Dockers. He was gagged and his arms and ankles were tied to the chair with ropes. Hannah had a flashback to several months ago, when the serial killer, Xander Thurman, had put her in the exact same position.

"What is this?" she asked slowly.

"It's a second chance," Bolton said with a chipperness that didn't fit the moment. "But before I explain further, you'll need to give me a moment."

Then he removed a large hypodermic needle from a bag at his feet and, without preamble, jammed it into the man's neck. Hannah gasped. Almost immediately, the man's eyes popped open. He made a desperate attempt to suck in air. But with the gag, he found it difficult and ended up coughing violently for a good fifteen seconds.

"This," Bolton said with an elaborate hand flourish, "is Robert Wilford Rylance. But his friends, to the extent that he has friends, call him Rob. Have you ever heard of him, Miss Hannah?"

Hannah shook her head. The man began to struggle at his ropes.

"That's okay," he continued, untroubled. "There's no reason you should have. Robert, Rob, I personally prefer Robbie—is a programmer for a well-known gaming company in Ontario. He's also a pedophile who traffics in child pornography. Isn't that right, Robbie?"

Robbie stopped struggling for a second, long enough to look over at Hannah pleadingly as he shook his head.

"They always deny it," Bolton said in his unhurried southern drawl. "But the physical evidence is overwhelming. This is what I found in files on his computer."

He tossed a sheaf of papers onto the floor in front of Hannah. They scattered but several small figures were clearly visible. Hannah could only look for a second before she turned away, gagging. The images bored into her skull, as awful as the sight of her own parents being slaughtered right in front of her. She tried to shut out what she'd seen, clenching her eyes shut tight. But it was too late. The memory of those children, even seen only fleetingly, would be there forever.

"I'm sorry," she heard Bolton say softly. "I'm sorry to have shown you that. I've made killing people my life's work and even I find this sort of thing distasteful. I can honestly say that among the dozens of people I've cut down, none has been a child. And I would certainly never consider doing . . . those things to an innocent. But I felt you had to know what we're dealing with here. You had to understand fully before I gave you this opportunity."

"What opportunity?" she finally managed to get out, despite the bile in her mouth.

"The opportunity to right this wrong; to bring righteous vengeance upon this perpetrator; to rid the world of a creature so vile that he doesn't deserve to draw breath. In short, Miss Hannah, I'm giving you the opportunity to end him."

With that, he removed a second item from the bag at his feet. It was a long hunting knife. He turned it over slowly. The blade gleamed in the overhead light.

"We both know that justice is hard to come by in this world," Bolton continued. "You know it better than most, Miss Hannah. It's rare that one gets a chance to so completely right a wrong. And I can't pretend this justice is complete. The children Robbie hurt in the past will suffer until they leave this world. We can't prevent that. But we can stop him from subjecting other little ones to the same fate. We can salvage the future of untold youngsters he might otherwise destroy. We can do that, Miss Hannah. You can do that."

"How?" she asked, though she already knew his answer.

"Simply take the knife and do what needs to be done."

Robbie looked at the knife and then at Hannah. His eyes were bulging now and he was yelling through his gag, though his words were unintelligible. He was shaking his head violently and rocking back and forth in his chair. The force of one particularly aggressive rock sent him careening backward and he slammed to the floor. Hannah heard his head hit with a thud.

That seemed to momentarily stun him as he didn't struggle when Bolton, after placing the knife on the ground, lifted the chair back upright. Hannah stared at the weapon, unable to pull her eyes away from it.

"It's beautiful in some terrible way, isn't it?" Bolton said, watching her. "Full of majestic violence. It's time to embrace the justice it can provide."

He picked up the knife and held it out to her.

Robbie was starting to regain his equilibrium again. He looked at her. He was no longer struggling against the ropes but his eyes were filled with confusion and fear. Something stirred inside her. It took her a moment to identify it as an unusual combination of satisfaction and pity. She chose to focus on the latter.

"I can't do it," she finally said.

Bolton stared at her for a long second, then pulled the knife away. He seemed truly disappointed.

"I understand," he said sympathetically. "It's a burden to do the hard work of striking down the wicked. Perhaps I expected too much of you. Sometimes knowing the right path and taking the first step on it are very different things. So I will take up this burden for you . . . this time."

Then, without another word, he turned to Robbie and pushed the knife into the right side of his stomach. He did it slowly and casually, like he was closing a troublesome dresser drawer that needed an extra shove.

Robbie's face widened in surprise at the unannounced action, then erupted into agony. Hannah heard a muffled scream escape his lips, before it turned into a long moan. Bolton removed the knife, looked at the deep red stain along the blade, and wiped it clean on Robbie's jeans.

Then he jammed the knife in again, this time a little harder. It entered right above Robbie's belly button. Bolton left it there, staring as it rose and fell with each increasingly labored breath from Robbie. Hannah turned away.

"Keep watching, Miss Hannah," Bolton instructed firmly. "Or you'll miss the most important part."

Despite her desperate desire not to, she returned her gaze to the scene in front of her. Robbie was breathing only intermittently now. Blood poured freely from his stomach and his eyes were getting dull.

"Here it comes," Bolton said with awe in his voice. "Watch for it. Watch for the moment when his life force leaves his body. Allow yourself to feel it enter ours."

And then it happened. Robbie's eyes turned glassy and his body slumped over, just as her foster father's had.

"I know that was hard, Miss Hannah," Bolton said gently. "But it was for the good. It had to be done. Now allow yourself to feel his life force become ours. Allow his energy to enter our cells."

But Hannah didn't feel any life force enter her.

All she felt was sick.

CHAPTER SIXTEEN

Jessie was faking it.

It was her job to always have something to go on. If not a hard lead, at least some sense of the motivation and mindset of the person she was after.

But as she stood in the District on the Bloc bar at the Sheraton Tower Hotel, waiting to talk to her second bartender of the night, Jessie had the distinct impression that most of what she'd surmised about Blue Eyes was what the killer wanted her to think. She had no confidence that the profile she was building was even close to accurate.

So she was faking it, pretending she had a strong sense of the woman in the hope that it might actually eventually prove true. She knew Ryan could see through the charade. But everyone else seemed to be buying it, which gave her a little space to operate. She took advantage of that space to review what they knew.

"So," she said to herself as much Ryan, "based on the surveillance video, it doesn't look like she followed the same routine as last time."

"Right," he agreed. "This time she hooked up with the victim in the same hotel where he picked her up rather than having them meet up at a second one later. What does that mean? Why would she change things up?"

Jessie had been wondering the same thing. Only minutes earlier, they'd reviewed the footage from the security office. To their surprise, they found that Blue Eyes had been loitering in the bar since about 8:30 p.m. Furthermore, based on their body language, it was pretty clear that she and Schumacher hadn't met before he tapped her shoulder in the bar.

Of course, just as confounding as the inconsistent methods Blue Eyes seemed to be using to snag her victims was the inconsistency of her appearance. Had they not seen Schumacher on the video talking to her in the bar, they wouldn't have realized that she was Blue Eyes at all.

Her hair was long and raven black. Unlike the comparatively demure dress that she wore with Gordon Maines, the one she had on tonight was much more revealing, with a plunging neckline and a slit nearly up to her hip. It was also a much bolder color—bright yellow instead of the more muted violet she wore the last time.

Jessie wondered if she was changing up her look based on the type of guy that frequented the bar. The Gallery Bar, where she'd met Maines, catered to a more conservative, professional crowd—bankers and political types. This one attracted a younger set with lots of models, actors, agents—all more drawn to shiny objects. If so, it suggested an even greater level of cunning than Jessie already credited her with.

"Jessie," Ryan repeated, snapping her out of her thoughts, "do you have any guesses as to why she would kill the guy in the same hotel where she met him? It seems reckless to me."

"I'm not sure," she admitted. "She was so patient last time. Maybe her taste for killing has escalated beyond her ability to control it."

"Maybe that's why she got rid of the blonde wig," he suggested. "She's not as interested in hiding her identity anymore."

"That could be it," she agreed. "But remember, she wore gloves the whole time. If she didn't care about her identity being revealed, why do that?"

Before they could continue the conversation, the bartender walked over. The guy projected an entirely different vibe from Brad. He was older— probably mid-thirties—and had the beginnings of gray in his black hair, which he made no effort to hide. He wore jeans and a worn, collared shirt, a far more casual look than the bar's patrons. He was good-looking in a rough, unfussy way that Jessie suspected worked a spell on many of the female customers.

"I'm Nick," he said, extending his hand to each of them. "My manager said you have some questions for me."

"Thanks for making the time," Ryan said.

"No problem. I was due for a break and I was told this took priority anyway."

"Right," Jessie said, pulling up her phone with the footage the security office had sent her. "We wanted you to look at some surveillance video from earlier tonight and tell us what you remember about these people."

She unpaused the clip a few seconds before Schumacher approached Blue Eyes and tapped her on the shoulder. They spoke for a minute before she gestured for him to take the unoccupied seat next to her.

"Okay," Nick said, without prompting. "The guy is Devin. I forget his last name—Schuman, Schuster—something like that. He's an agent at some big Hollywood firm, works out of their satellite office downtown."

"I feel like you're holding back, Nick," Jessie said, sensing the guy had more to share.

"Well, there's also the fact that he's an asshole, and not just because he's a crappy tipper. He's grabby when he's drunk, sometimes even when he's sober. He also got into at least two shoving matches that I can think of. I've had to threaten to kick him out a couple of times because of complaints."

"And the girl?" Ryan asked.

"I've seen her around but only a few times. I think she's new to town."

"Why do you say that?" Jessie asked.

"Hard to explain. Just a feeling. After doing this job for so long, you just get a sense of people. She didn't seem sure of herself or her surroundings, although that could just be because she was new to the bar."

"Did you see her interact with other folks before tonight?" Ryan asked.

"Sure," Nick answered with a jaded look. "I don't want to cast aspersions. But I'm pretty sure she was a working girl."

"What makes you think that?" Jessie pressed.

"Part of it is like my guess about her not being local; just a vibe. But also, she never came with friends, always alone. She always paid cash. She always left with a man, invariably one who had money to spare. And she had a very businesslike demeanor about her. She didn't seem nervous, like the girls who are hoping to meet a cool guy. She seemed like she was . . . doing a job."

"Could she have not been nervous because she was confident that she could meet anyone she wanted?" Ryan asked. "She *is* pretty attractive."

"That's understating it," Nick replied. "The video doesn't do her justice. She's breathtaking, especially with those blue eyes. They're magnetic. But in my experience, and as I'm sure your partner there can tell you, even the most beautiful woman in a room can feel self-conscious. She didn't seem to have that issue. And I think it's because she probably wasn't looking for a boyfriend. She was looking for a payday. That eliminates a lot of the insecurity."

"Did you ever talk to her?"

"Only in passing. I served her tonight, as you can see from the video. She nursed one drink the whole time she was here so I didn't focus on her much. It gets pretty crazy in here so long conversations are hard to come by and she didn't seem interested in those anyway. I think she called herself Lexi. Maybe it was Sexy? That's a little on the nose, right? Either way, if I'm right about her line of work, I'd be surprised if that was her real name anyway."

Jessie tended to agree.

"Anything else you can recall?" Ryan asked.

"Not really. But if the rumors I'm hearing are true, you've got your work cut out for you."

"What rumors?" Ryan asked.

Nick shrugged.

"Word gets around," he said. "And the word is someone killed Devin. If that's true, I wouldn't just point the finger at a possible escort he met in a bar. He was the kind of guy who lots of folks would have happily killed if they thought they could get away with it."

"Should we count you among them?" Ryan asked, his eyebrow raised.

"Nah," Nick said. "He was actually good for my business. Other folks saw what a jerk he was to the bar staff and gave us sympathy tips. It was almost worth putting up with him for that. Are we good? I can see that our other bartender is starting to get swamped."

Jessie couldn't think of any other questions. Ryan looked satisfied too.

"We're good for now," he said, handing over his card. "Just make sure to call if you see her again. Obviously, she's dangerous."

Nick nodded and hurried back behind the bar. Ryan turned to Jessie.

"I've got a sinking feeling Blue Eyes was long gone before we got here."

"Should we lift the lockdown?" she asked.

"Yeah. We can leave a couple of officers at the various entrances but I suspect even that's a waste of time."

"Speaking of time," she said, "how do you suggest we utilize ours?"

"I was thinking we should pay a visit to Devin Schumacher's fiancée. Someone needs to make the notification and I'd rather it be us than some uniformed officer."

"Out of the kindness of your heart?" Jessie asked skeptically.

"I think we both know it's out of the suspicion of my heart. I want to see her face when we tell her. We may have our suspect but her motive is still unknown. There's still the chance that she's a killer for hire. I want to know if Devin's bride-to-be had a reason to want him killed."

"You know it's almost midnight, right?" Jessie pointed out. "We're going to show up at a woman's home after midnight to tell her that her fiancé was found dead and naked in a hotel room?"

"I find that I often get people's most genuine reactions when they're tired, stressed, or both."

Jessie tended to agree. In fact, she might add one more truth-detector to the mix: anger. And before she could stop herself, a nasty thought popped into her head.

Maybe pissing off Devin's fiancée is our quickest route to the truth.

CHAPTER SEVENTEEN

Jessie hated to tarnish the beauty of the evening.

As they drove to the Hollywood Hills home that Devin Schumacher shared with his fiancée, Deborah Morse, she marveled at the twinkling lights of the homes against the night sky. From a distance, it looked like they were embedded into the hills themselves, like permanent Christmas ornaments draping a massive tree.

But soon, for one woman at least, all that beauty would quickly fade. Jessie felt her spine stiffen in anticipation of what she was about to do. If Deborah Morse was truly a grieving woman, that would be hard enough. But if she was something more sinister, Jessie had to be on guard for that too.

They pulled up to the home, which looked modest from the driveway. But as Jessie knew, most of these houses were much bigger in the back, expanding down the hillside with three, sometimes four floors. She doubted this would be the exception.

Ryan rang the doorbell. They waited silently for any reaction from within. Jessie looked at the time: 12:24 a.m. No surprise that it was taking a while. Ryan rang the bell a second time and knocked loudly.

"How long should we give her?" he asked.

Jessie was mildly amused by his impatience.

"A while, Ryan. If she was asleep, it's going to take a few minutes for her to get herself together. Plus, she might be a little apprehensive about answering the door, considering the hour."

"So two minutes?" he said, feigning denseness.

"Who is it?" a sleepy, annoyed female voice asked from the decrepit-looking intercom that Jessie had incorrectly assumed didn't work.

"We're with the LAPD, Ms. Morse," Ryan said, his tone becoming instantly somber. "We need to speak with you."

"What is this about?" the voice asked, still annoyed but much less sleepy now.

"Please come to the door, ma'am. We need to speak to you in person."

"How do I know this isn't some kind of scam to get in and rob or rape me?" she demanded.

Jessie fought the urge to roll her eyes. Instead she responded as calmly as she could.

"We're not here to rape you, Ms. Morse. My name is Jessie Hunt. I'm a criminal profiler with the LAPD. I'm here with Detective Ryan Hernandez. If you want, you can call the department. We'll hold up our badges and you can verify the numbers with them if you like. But we really need to speak with you."

"Why are the police at my front door at twelve thirty in the morning?"

"It's about Devin," Jessie finally said, realizing that unless she cut to the chase, this process could take ten minutes. They needed to gauge her reaction to the news of his death in real time, not after she'd had a chance to prepare herself.

"Give me a minute," Deborah said. The line went dead.

Jessie looked over at Ryan.

"Sorry," she said sheepishly. "I didn't think we had a choice."

"You were probably right to mention him. Don't sweat it. We can't wait out here all night."

A minute later, they heard scuffling on the other side of the door.

"Show me your badges, please," Deborah asked with considerably less irritation than before.

They did. Seconds later they heard multiple locks being undone. The door opened to reveal a smallish woman around Jessie's age. She had dirty-blonde hair pulled back in a ponytail and wore a robe.

"What did he do now?" she asked before either of them got a word out. "Is he in the drunk tank again? Busted for solicitation? Assault? I'm not bailing him out this time!"

"Has your fiancé been arrested often?" Ryan asked.

Jessie could tell he was kicking himself for not checking the guy's record earlier. But she had made the same mistake. They were both so focused on the killer that they hadn't looked into the victim's background thoroughly. Admittedly, they'd been working this case for over fourteen hours and were operating on fumes. But that was no excuse.

"Is four times since we started dating often? I don't even know what's normal anymore."

"He hasn't been arrested," Ryan said, clearly deciding to direct the conversation away from their professional screw-up.

He glanced over at Jessie to let her know he was about to drop the hammer so that she could watch Deborah closely. She nodded and he turned back to Deborah.

"Ms. Morse," he said. "I'm sorry to inform you that Devin is dead."

She stared at him for a few seconds, as if she hadn't actually processed his words. She rubbed her eyes as if that might help give her greater clarity of mind.

"I'm sorry. What did you say?"

"Devin passed away earlier this evening," Ryan repeated, revealing as few details as possible.

"That's not possible," Deborah said without confidence, now turning to Jessie. "How is that possible?"

"I'm afraid it's true, Ms. Morse," Jessie said as soothingly as possible. "His body was discovered about three hours ago."

Just as Margo Maines had done, Deborah Morse reached out and gripped the doorframe.

"I need to sit down," she said, sounding cloudy. "Is it okay if I sit down?"

"Of course," Jessie told her. "We can help you back inside."

"Here is good," she said and slumped down on the front step.

Jessie looked over at Ryan, unsure how hard she should push at the moment. He shrugged, as if to say "you're the profiler lady." She gave him a glare and knelt down next to Deborah.

"I know this is a lot to process, Deborah. But we need to ask you some questions while everything is fresh. Your input could be crucial to resolving the case."

"What case?" Deborah asked, seeming to slightly regroup. "How did he die? Was he killed?"

"It's too early to draw definitive conclusions," Jessie hedged. "But we have to consider all options. You mentioned that he'd been taken in for both solicitation and assault. Do you know if anyone involved in those prior situations had expressed animosity toward Devin?"

Deborah stared absently into space. Jessie was about to rephrase her question when the woman looked up at her. Her eyes were clear and more than slightly angry.

"I have no idea. From what he told me, the fights were mostly drunken brawls with strangers in bars. The women he was with? We didn't really talk about that very much and I was fine with that."

"Does this woman look familiar?" Jessie asked, showing her the screen grab of Blue Eyes with dark hair.

Deborah looked at the image, squinting as if that might help.

"I don't know," she finally said. "I mean, should it?"

"You sound pretty blasé about your fiancé's indiscretions," Ryan said, unable to hide the surprise in his voice.

Deborah tossed him a weary glare that suggested he was far from the first person to make this point.

"Thanks for sharing, Detective," she said acidly. "Listen, Devin is hardly perfect. But he's funny and passionate and real, which is hard to say about most guys I've dated in Los Angeles. He's from a small town in Ohio, and you could tell. He wasn't cynical about everything. At least he didn't used to be. Anyway, he assured me he was going to clean up his act. And if he didn't, there was always the prenup."

"The prenup?" Jessie nudged, noting that Deborah was still referring to her fiancé in the present tense.

"Yeah. My father insisted on it and frankly, so did I. My family is fairly well off. Devin's finances are more … in flux. He's actually on a fixed allowance that we set up. And the prenup papers are iron-clad. Any infidelity is cause for divorce and he gets nothing. Any arrest on a charge related to prior charges is cause for divorce and he gets nothing. He has to submit to monthly STD checkups and quarterly blood work. Any unsatisfying results are cause … you get the idea."

"So it's safe to assume that he wasn't sitting on a massive nest egg?" Ryan asked.

Deborah looked at him like the question was crazy.

"If you're asking if this was my doing as some way to get all of Devin's money, that's laughable. He's a good talent agent, but at this stage of his career, he's still scraping by. He'd be lucky to pull two hundred fifty grand this year. The allowance I give him is more than that. He didn't have any life insurance policy. And we're not married yet anyway, so I don't see how I could have collected, even if he did."

Jessie and Ryan exchanged a glance that suggested they were thinking the same thing. Apparently, to Deborah Morse, $250,000 was a mere pittance. Neither mentioned it.

"Do you know his phone password?" Ryan asked. "Quickly accessing his texts, calls, and location data could be very helpful in discerning how this happened, and why."

Deborah gave it to them and then asked them the question Jessie had been dreading.

"Now what?"

Ryan was prepared for it.

"We have a squad car en route. If you could get dressed, they'll take you down to the medical examiner's office to identify the body and collect his belongings. We may have more questions for you in the morning. But for now, that's your only responsibility."

They joined her inside while she changed. No one said it but they were also there to keep an eye out for any suspicious behavior. As she loitered near Morse's bedroom, Jessie couldn't wait for the uniformed officers to arrive.

After her first full day on the job in over a week, her body was exhausted and her brain was mush. She needed a few hours of sleep to regroup and determine their next course of action.

The lab reports on possible evidence, including blood work on Schumacher and prints and possible trace DNA, would be in by then. Surveillance footage from near the hotel might offer some help. She wasn't optimistic but it was possible.

Hell, anything is possible. Maybe by tomorrow Blue Eyes will have turned herself in. Maybe Garland Moses will have gotten a break in Hannah's case. Maybe Hannah herself will be waiting for me in the station bullpen after escaping from Crutchfield.

The fact that Jessie could allow herself to believe any of that was credible was the surest sign that she was done for the night. When the uniformed officers finally arrived at close to one a.m., she headed straight to the car. She was asleep before Ryan put the vehicle in drive.

CHAPTER EIGHTEEN

A lex Cutter hid behind a dumpster.

She waited for the sirens to fade into the distance. But just as they did, a new round started up, even closer than the last. She pulled off her brunette wig and tossed it in the dumpster. She would have preferred to just shove it in her bag, but if she was caught with it, there'd be no explaining it away. At least now, her real, short-cropped blonde hair wouldn't match any footage from the hotel.

Devin Schumacher had really screwed her.

As she knelt by the trash receptacle, trying not to gag on the scents emanating from it, she seethed silently. All her hard work over the last few weeks had been put at risk by one picture frame falling off a wall. It didn't seem fair, considering all the time and preparation it had taken. She still remembered the crucial moment back in Las Vegas when she'd decided to take charge of her own life.

It took a few months before she killed again. For a long time she coasted on the sense of self-determination that came from fighting back against Dan. But after a while, she began to understand that it wasn't fighting back that had energized her, it was the power she had over him as she beat him into a fleshy mess that gave her the rush.

She had so rarely experienced that power. And as she resumed her normal life, fulfilling the desires of her tricks, that power started to dissipate. She grew to miss it and then to think about it all the time. It became all-consuming.

She believed that, if she was careful, she could catch lightning in a bottle twice. After all, no one suspected a thing. The news reports about Dan's death all described it as a robbery gone wrong. There was no mention of a woman or of any leads. It was possible that the police were keeping some details to themselves. But for now, the coast appeared clear.

So Alex started to plan the next one. She selected a client, a doctor named Harvey who was also a raging alcoholic. He was sometimes violent in their encounters and almost always verbally abusive. But he was no worse than many others and if he'd been a real estate agent or an architect instead of a physician, he likely would have been safe.

But Alex told the doctor a sob story about a few awful dates she'd had where being able to drug the john and sneak out would have been a blessing. She offered to give him a month's worth of freebies if he delivered her a year's supply of powerful sedatives. She made the request when he was drunk. But truthfully, he didn't take much convincing.

His only requirement was that as part of the deal, they had to have their next date at the Venetian on the strip. He said he'd use the money he wouldn't have to spend on her for the next month on a suite.

Alex was reluctant because of all the cameras and security at the Venetian. But he was adamant. So, in the days leading up to the date she scouted the hotel in various disguises, learning the location of the cameras and where the security officers liked to set up position.

On the day of the date, she called Harvey on a burner phone and said she'd be wearing a special costume. She told him to take a seat at the Dorsey Cocktail Bar at nine o'clock and she'd find him. He seemed excited by the prospect.

When she sat down next to him that night, in a red wig and floral sundress, he didn't even recognize her. She had to lean in and whisper something dirty in his ear before he realized it was her. Then she sent him up to the suite, where she met him fifteen minutes later.

There was a point where she reconsidered. After he gave her the supply of sedatives, along with a diamond necklace, she wondered if perhaps she could choose another victim. But her second thoughts went away when he showed her the toys he planned to use on her that night. None of them were designed for her pleasure; in fact, quite the opposite.

Besides, if she let him go and drugged other johns, he might figure it out. He might go to the cops. He was a loose end that needed to be clipped. In retrospect, it was odd how easy the premeditated decision to kill another human being, even one as unpleasant as Harvey, had been.

Her mind made up, Alex sent him to the bathroom to shower so she could "get comfortable." While he was in the bathroom, she got a drink from the mini-bar for him (he liked vodka and cranberry). She added a massive dose of lorazepam, which conveniently enough, was even more effective when paired with alcohol.

When he came into the room, dressed only in a towel, she handed him the drink, wearing a pair of elbow-length white gloves that he noticed and called "sexy." She told him to enjoy his drink while she freshened up.

She waited five minutes. When she returned to the room, she feared something had gone wrong. The glass was empty but Harvey was sitting at the foot of the bed, looking as alert as ever.

"Ready, lover?" she asked, hiding her apprehension.

It was only when he tried to speak that Alex knew it had worked. He looked at her and opened his mouth. But instead of words, only garbled grumbles came out. She thought she heard the words "dose me" but couldn't be certain. Regardless, the panicked look in his eyes told her he understood what she'd done.

Suddenly, the tingling, floating sensation she'd felt in the aftermath of Dan's death, the one that had faded in recent months, returned with a vengeance.

It was like *she'd* been dosed with some kind of drug. It was magical.

But now, Devin Schumacher's druggy clumsiness had undermined both her carefully constructed plan and the adrenaline rush she so coveted. The second he knocked over the picture frame and it shattered on the floor, she knew the clock was ticking.

It was possible that the rooms near her were unoccupied. But she couldn't count on it. Assuming there were guests next door and they were nosy, she had estimated she had about ten minutes before someone from the hotel checked up on them. To be safe, she gave herself half that.

As a result, the Reckoning, as she'd grown fond of calling it, was rushed and unsatisfying.

She did get a little thrill when Schumacher made a feeble attempt to shove her away. Something about him fighting back was especially yummy. Slapping his face had given her a satisfying, if brief, tingle of delight.

The actual strangling was a bit of a letdown. She still got that adrenaline hit of watching his body writhe and his eyes bulge as she wrung the life out of him. But it was slightly dulled by the constant worry that at any moment, someone might knock on the door.

Worse than that, she had to begin the wrap-up process almost immediately. There was no chance to linger over her accomplishment, to revel in the elimination of another threat to her, to all women. With Harvey, the Las Vegas doctor, and with Gordon Maines, she'd had time to imagine it was her stepfather lying naked and helpless on the bed. But Schumacher had deprived her of that opportunity.

She would need to remedy that. As she walked casually down the street, making her way to the dingy, week-to-week hotel room she'd called home for the last few months, an idea emerged.

She would go out again tomorrow night. She knew she shouldn't. She knew they'd be looking for her. But she didn't have a choice. The buzz she'd been anticipating, the one she deserved, had been stolen from her. She wanted it back.

Besides, it might actually be better to have one last Reckoning tomorrow, before the cops had a chance to come up with a plan. Right now they'd be scrambling, trying to figure out her patterns, trying to identify her. If she gave them extra days, they might come across some mistake she'd made.

But if she did it in the next twenty-four hours, she could slip through their grasp. She'd have one last perfect evening and then go dark for a while, move to a different city where there wasn't as much heat. She'd always wanted to visit San Francisco or maybe Seattle.

But before that, there was work to do.

CHAPTER NINETEEN

When Jessie woke up in the middle of the night, she found she was lying in her own bed without any recollection of how she got there. Ryan must have carried her up from the car. She must have really been wiped out not to remember any of that.

She rolled over and tried to go back to sleep. But unwanted thoughts forced their way into her head. She began to think of Blue Eyes, or Lexi, as she apparently called herself. Maybe there was some significance to that name. She'd have to investigate the possibility in the morning.

Her thoughts then turned to Hannah, wondering what was happening to her at this moment. Was she asleep? Was Crutchfield depriving her of it in order to wear her down?

Realizing she wasn't going to be able to drift off again, Jessie got up to go to the kitchen for a glass of water. The second she stepped out of her bedroom, she knew something was off. As part of the security measures to keep her safe, Ryan typically slept on the pull-out sofa. But it wasn't pulled out and he was nowhere to be found. Did he decide not to stay tonight? Even if he had left, one of the protective officers would have been assigned to take his place. Something was wrong.

"Ryan?" she whispered.

There was no answer. She glanced back to her room and saw her cell phone resting on the side table. Her gun was kept in the drawer below. She started to take a step back into the room when she heard a throat clear. She recognized the voice even before he spoke.

"No, Miss Jessie, it's not Ryan. I'm afraid he's indisposed at the moment."

Bolton Crutchfield stepped into the living room from the hall, the half light from the moon illuminating him and someone else, whom he was holding in front of him. It was Hannah, clearly exhausted and being physically held up by Crutchfield. She was gagged. He pressed a long knife to her throat.

"Let her go," Jessie ordered with more steeliness than she thought possible.

"I'm afraid I can't do that, Miss Jessie. As you know, I've been conducting an experiment of sorts. Unfortunately, your little sister here failed. So now I'm making you my test subject. You have a choice. I can slit young Hannah's throat and then leave. I will never bother you again. Or you can sacrifice yourself for her and I will let her go, to lead a hopefully long life, though likely not one devoid of emotional trauma. The choice is yours."

Then he removed the gag from Hannah's mouth. The girl tried to swallow. Her throat was clearly dry and she was having trouble speaking. When she finally managed to get words out, they were few but pointed.

"Please save me."

"Now you know where she stands," Crutchfield said, chuckling. "The choice is yours. But considering the lateness of the hour and the chances that we'll soon have company, I can only give you, let's say ... seven seconds to decide."

Of course, for Jessie it was no decision at all.

"Seven, six ..."

Without time to get to a gun or a phone, she could only offer herself up in a trade. There was no way she would let Hannah die.

"Five, four ..."

Maybe once the girl was free and clear, she could call for help. Maybe Jessie could outfight Crutchfield. At least that way, there was a chance.

"Three, two ..."

"Please!" Hannah screamed.

Jessie opened her mouth to offer herself up, to take Hannah's place, to die in her stead. But no words came out. She tried to speak but it was as if her vocal cords had been cut out. There was nothing but a soft rasp.

"One, zero ..."

She held up her hand to indicate that he should stop, that she agreed to his terms. He smiled, his uneven teeth gleaming in the moonlight.

"Sorry, Miss Jessie. You dillied and you dallied. And now it's too late."

With that, he raised the knife and sliced it across the front of Hannah's throat. Her scream turned into a gurgle as blood spewed everywhere, spraying Jessie in the face.

Jessie wanted to scream "no," to run forward. But she seemed frozen in place without any ability to speak.

Hannah's eyes, filled with pain and accusation, grew wide, then quickly dulled. Crutchfield let go of her and she dropped to the ground with a thud.

⚜ ⚜ ⚜

Jessie bolted upright in bed and nearly toppled to the floor. The door swung open and Ryan rushed in. She heard screaming nearby and realized that it was her.

"What is it?" Ryan asked. "Are you okay?"

Jessie swiveled her head around the bedroom. There was no one else there. Morning sunlight was streaming in. Her whole body was coated in sweat.

"It was so real," she managed to mutter, before she started shivering involuntarily. She felt her body heaving and realized she was sobbing.

Ryan grabbed a bed sheet and draped it over her. He didn't say anything. Instead he simply wrapped his arms around her and pulled her in tight. And that was enough for now.

CHAPTER TWENTY

Jessie was embarrassed.

She had told Ryan about the dream, but by the time they arrived at the station later that morning, she almost wished she hadn't. He'd seen her in such a raw, vulnerable moment that now, whenever he looked at her, she felt as if she no longer had any protective shell.

He must have sensed her disquiet because he didn't say anything about what had happened, sticking only to banal pleasantries. When they walked into the bullpen after making a coffee and muffin pit stop in the kitchen, they found Captain Decker waiting for them by their desks in the bullpen with his arms crossed and an impatient expression.

Captain Roy Decker, who ran Central Station, was a few months shy of sixty but looked a decade older. Bald, save for a few sad, lonely tufts, he was skinny and sunken faced, with wrinkles that seemed chiseled into his forehead. His beady eyes were hawk-like, as was his long, pointed nose. He looked like an old but still dangerous bird of prey.

"Hernandez, Hunt," he began without preamble, "I have updates for you on the hotel murders. Care to join me in my office?"

It wasn't really a request so they followed him and sat down as he closed the door behind them. He moved over to his immaculate desk and sat down, studying them both silently before he began.

"First," he said with an air of obligation, "it's good to have you back, Hunt. I'm sorry I didn't see you yesterday and get to welcome you back then. I know it was difficult to take a week's leave when you didn't think you needed it. But department policy required it and I appreciate you not pushing on the matter."

"Yes, sir," Jessie said, getting the distinct impression that he was being nicer than usual because he was about to drop some bad news on her.

"Before we discuss this case, I wanted to update you on the Dorsey girl. I'm sure you have questions. As you know well, the FBI has taken over the investigation of her abduction and the murder of her foster parents. They are being tight-lipped about it. But I do know that they've confirmed Crutchfield was the abductor based on fingerprints on the knives used in the murders."

"We already knew that, sir," Jessie said, frustrated.

"Yes, but they confirmed it. And they shared that detail. That's more than we usually get."

"So they confirmed a fact we had already established?" Ryan noted. "Is that supposed to be progress?"

"For the FBI, yes," Decker answered.

"Do they have any leads on where he might have taken Hannah?" Jessie asked, trying to stick to the most crucial point.

"Nothing they're willing to share," Decker admitted.

"And they're still not interested in having the assistance of the criminal profiler who knows more than anyone about how Crutchfield thinks?" Ryan asked, glancing over at Jessie.

"Not at this time," Decker said, clearly equally annoyed but unable to say it. "So let's move on to the other case."

"That's it?" Jessie asked. "We're done with Hannah?"

"Certainly *you* are," Decker said in warning tone. "They don't want you anywhere near that case. You know the consequences for ignoring that order are severe. I know it's frustrating but we're hamstrung here. So let's address the hotel murders, shall we?"

"Yes sir," Jessie said reluctantly.

"Overnight, the lab was able to confirm that Schumacher was drugged with lorazepam, the same sedative used on Gordon Maines. Unfortunately, as with Maines, there was no usable physical evidence. The killer used gloves. There were no fingerprints and no worthwhile DNA samples. It looks like she didn't just wipe the room down. She also sprayed it with a powerful antiseptic disinfecting agent that degrades everything. Tech is very frustrated, and not just because of that."

"What else?" Ryan asked.

"They've gone over the surveillance from the hotel and the surrounding area. It looks like killer went into a staff restroom, left wearing a hooded sweatshirt, and then proceeded to exit through a service door along with multiple kitchen staffers who had just clocked out. Cameras on the surrounding streets lost her in the crowd."

"So we're back to square one?" Jessie said.

"It's worse than that," Decker said with an apprehensiveness that told Jessie this was the bad news he'd been holding back when he was being nice to her earlier.

"What?" she asked.

"The FBI's taking over this case too," he said flatly.

"What!" both Jessie and Ryan yelled in unison.

Decker waited a moment for them to settle before continuing.

"They've determined that these murders bear a strong similarity to one that took place in Las Vegas a few months ago. A doctor was drugged, robbed, and strangled at the Venetian on the Strip. And since we seem to be looking at a serial killer murdering people in multiple states, it's now a federal case and they want it."

"When are they taking over?" Ryan asked.

"Three hours. Two agents from the Vegas field office are en route now. When they arrive, it will officially become an FBI matter. So I recommend you use the intervening time to catch up on all the details so you can thoroughly brief them upon their arrival. Do you understand?"

"Yes sir," Ryan said before Jessie could respond. "We'll get right on that."

She noticed that he sounded less demoralized that she felt. He cast her a knowing look and motioned for them to leave. Decker said nothing as they departed his office.

"What was that all about?" she asked, confused.

Ryan looked at her with unexpected excitement.

"You haven't known Decker as long as I have," he said. "So there's no way you could have picked up on it. But he was giving us a green light to keep investigating."

"He was?" Jessie frowned. "I didn't get that at all. It sounded like he was telling us to steer clear."

"That's what it sounded like. And that's what he'll say if pressed. But think about it. He basically told us the FBI will be taking over in three hours and that we have until then to investigate so we can properly 'brief' them. That means that we have three hours until we have to hand the case over. Until then, it's still ours."

They decided to use the time to look into the Vegas doctor murder and see if they could uncover any connections that would help. They had just started reviewing the case file when Jessie got a call. It was Garland Moses.

"I have to take this," she told Ryan as she hurried out of the bullpen. "I'll be right back."

He looked at her curiously but said nothing.

"Hey, Garland," she said when she found a private corner of the courtyard. "I could really use some good news."

"Good morning to you too, Hunt," he replied.

"Sorry," she said. "It's already been a challenging one. And I'm tight on time with the case I'm working."

"That's actually what I wanted to tell you about."

"My case—the hotel murders?" she said, surprised. "Not the other thing?"

"Your case," he said. "I may have a lead for you."

"Really," Jessie asked, pulling out her notebook. "Okay, shoot."

"A man went missing yesterday out in Redlands. He may be a victim of your serial killer."

That didn't sound right to Jessie.

"Both our victims were found downtown," she pointed out. "Redlands is a good sixty-five to seventy miles away. What makes you think they're connected?"

"It's more of a gut feeling than any fact pattern," he admitted.

"Okay," Jessie said, more than a little confused. "What hotel was he at? And who's in charge of the case? I'll reach out."

There was a moment of hesitation on the other end of the line.

"That's the thing. He wasn't at a hotel and it's not formally a missing person case yet. He hasn't been missing for twenty-four hours so the investigation hasn't started yet. But the man's wife seems convinced that he was taken. She tried calling him but his phone was turned off along with the GPS."

Jessie was genuinely perplexed. This case, to the extent that it even was a case, sounded completely random.

"Garland, just to make sure I understand. You're telling me that a guy who lives over an hour out of LA and wasn't staying at a hotel, who hasn't answered his wife's calls and isn't even a formal missing person, is somehow a victim in my case and that that's what I should be pursuing in the limited time I have available."

"That's correct."

"And you won't tell me more than that?"

"I can give you his name."

Had it been anyone else, Jessie would have hung up by now. But this was Garland Moses, who was solving cases now taught in textbooks since before she was born. And he was telling her to follow this lead.

So she took down the name and thanked him.

Then she went to tell Ryan that, while he was looking for connections to the Vegas case, she was headed off on a wild goose chase.

CHAPTER TWENTY ONE

Jessie felt like she was driving straight into hell.

The route from Los Angeles to Redlands, California, was occasionally picturesque. But the last stretch of the nearly seventy-minute drive was a barren, ugly wasteland, comprised mostly of half-used quarries, abandoned mills, looming warehouses, and endless billboards for strip clubs.

When she finally arrived at the home of the supposed victim, she was mildly impressed to find a modest but well-kept ranch house in an unremarkable suburb. She was slightly ashamed to admit that she'd been expecting something closer to a ramshackle shed. But other than the chemical smell in the air and the non-stop sound of an industrial-strength jackhammer much too close to a neighborhood, the place seemed blandly respectable.

The wife of the missing man opened the door even before Jessie had a chance to knock. Her brown hair looked like a bird's nest and there were dark shadows under her eyes. She was wearing a bulky bathrobe that Jessie suspected was her husband's.

"Are you the one from LAPD that Mr. Moses mentioned?" she asked breathlessly.

"Yes, hi," Jessie said, extending her hand. "My name is Jessie Hunt."

"Please come in. I'm Victoria. Call me Vicky."

"Thank you, Vicky."

"Can I offer you some coffee, Ms. Hunt?"

"It's Jessie and no thanks. I can tell you're anxious so why don't we just cut to the chase? Why do you think your husband is missing?"

"I know the police think I'm overreacting," Vicky said, plopping down at the breakfast table. "But you have to understand that Bob leads a very well-ordered life. He wakes up every day at six. He runs on the treadmill for thirty-one minutes. He showers for six minutes. For breakfast every morning he has two eggs, scrambled, with shredded cheddar cheese and avocado slices, a piece of whole wheat toast, and a banana. He's always out the door by seven fifteen to make it to the office by eight. He leaves his desk at exactly five p.m. every day. And unless he's running an errand or has a meeting, he's home by five fifty-five. If he's going to be late, he calls. He considers lateness to be rude. If I call him and he can't answer, he always replies within five minutes. He considers non-responsiveness to be rude. Bob doesn't change it up. He isn't spontaneous. And he most certainly doesn't stay out all night without giving me a call. Plus his GPS is turned off, which it never is. And all my calls go straight to voicemail so I think his phone is off too."

Jessie sat quietly at the table for a minute, giving Vicky a chance to settle down. She got the impression that Bob wasn't the only one in the family who liked things orderly. When she thought Vicky had calmed down a bit, she replied.

"Is it possible that something happened that he might not be comfortable telling you about?"

"Like what?" Vicky asked sharply.

"If he got demoted or lost his job, maybe he was embarrassed and wasn't sure how to tell you. Maybe he's staying away to avoid sharing the news?"

Vicky's head was shaking before Jessie even finished the question.

"First of all, he's great at his job. He's been there over a decade and they love him. They offered him promotions twice and he turned them down because he likes the nitty-gritty of programming. Second, if he was fired, he wouldn't avoid my calls. He'd be mad. I work in HR and I know how to deal with that sort of thing. He'd want my help navigating the bureaucracy right away."

Okay," Jessie conceded. "Is there another reason he might be out of touch? Maybe he went out for drinks with friends, got drunk, and slept it off at someone's house?"

Vicky looked at her like she'd suggested that her husband had gone to the moon. She responded slowly and with certitude.

"Bob doesn't get drunk with friends. He isn't that kind of guy."

"What kind of guy is he?" Jessie asked carefully.

"He's the kind of guy who tithes ten percent to the church and works at the soup kitchen twice a week. He's the kind of guy who volunteers at the

Boys and Girls Clubs almost every weekend, teaching them how to code. He's a good man."

Jessie nodded. She didn't say so but for the first time since Garland Moses had suggested she check out this lead, her interest was piqued. Maybe it wasn't fair but anytime a wife said her husband was a good man, it gave her pause.

"Okay," she said, standing up. "I may have other questions for you later. But for now, I'm going to go the police department and see if I can get them to put some more resources into looking for Bob."

"Thank you," Vicky said. "But remember, I'm the only one who calls him Bob. They'll know him by his full name, Robert."

"Right," Jessie said, looking down at her notes. "I've got it. Robert Wilford Rylance."

Jessie tried not to make assumptions in her line of work.

But even before talking to Redlands Police Chief Dwayne Stoller, she knew he wasn't going to be much help.

He seemed interested when he first saw her, giving her a less than covert once-over as he introduced himself. But once they sat down in his office and she explained why she was there, his eyes glazed over right in front of her as she spoke. When he replied, he sounded annoyed that he had to offer any explanation at all.

"I told that woman she could file a missing person report at exactly six twenty-two p.m., twenty-four hours after she first called about him. She took the paperwork with her and has already filled it out. I fully expect to see her here at six tonight if her husband hasn't shown up by then, which I'm confident he will."

"Why is that?" she asked.

Chief Stoller adjusted his considerable weight in his creaky chair, pushed a strand of greasy black hair out his eye, and answered, his voice dripping with condescension.

"Look, Profiler Hunt," he said, nearly spitting out her title, "this sort of thing happens all the time."

"What sort of thing?" Jessie asked, forcing her own tone to stay detached and professional.

"We're not L.A. people. There are no Hollywood stars walking into our local Starbucks. There are no 'sweet' waves to surf. People get bored. Husbands especially get bored. Sometimes they pound a few brews and pass out. Sometimes they go the local casino and spend that week's salary at the blackjack table. Morongo Casino is only a half hour west of here. Maybe he was driving home, thought about spending the evening with Mrs. Rylance, and just kept going."

"Mrs. Rylance suggested that would be very out of character for her husband," Jessie said tightly.

"Who's to say what a person's real character is? Maybe that sort of thing isn't truly revealed until you're stuck in a traffic jam eastbound on the I-10. But I guess that's more your area of expertise, right, Profiler Hunt, understanding people's secret character? Speaking of, this seems like an awful small case for a big-time LAPD lady to be looking into. Is there something you're not telling me? Because if you say there's a credible reason I should move this 'case' to the front of the line when I have a huge backlog waiting for my attention, I'll gladly do it. Is there?"

Jessie thought fast. There really was no believable reason she could offer for him to take this case more seriously than he was. Despite Garland Moses's suggestion, there was nothing that seemed to even remotely link Robert Rylance to her hotel murders. And she doubted Chief Stoller was inclined to go out of his way for anyone based on a hunch.

"No, Chief," she finally said. "But I would appreciate it if you could locate his phone once his wife turns in that missing person report, maybe check his credit card purchases in the last day, even if that means moving his case ahead in line. Maybe you're right and they'll show him at the casino, in which case you can get Victoria Rylance off your back. And if it turns out that you find something unusual, I sure would appreciate a call. Consider it a favor, one that I'll gladly return when you're in need."

"You're offering me the fancy services of a big-time LA profiler lady? Be still my fat-clogged heart."

"I am," she said, refusing to say all the things that were currently popping into her head as she got up and extended her hand. "Thanks for your time, Chief."

She made sure to douse her hands in Purell once back in the car, refusing to imagine where Chief Stoller's had recently been. Once back on the road, she was tempted to call up Garland and ream him out for what seemed like an enormous, unproductive time suck. But she erred on the side of restraint. Maybe there was something she was missing. It wouldn't be the first time.

Still, it made no sense. Why would Lexi, in the middle of her downtown LA murder spree, take the time to drive out to nowhere to kidnap a guy who didn't fit her victim profile?

Robert Rylance wasn't rich or powerful. Based on the photos his wife showed her, he was just a pale, mildly schlubby computer programmer. He looked more like the kind of guy who got off playing video games than hiring a prostitute.

Then again, maybe Chief Stoller was right. Who knew how Rylance got his jollies? Maybe he *was* at a casino. Maybe he was at one of the strip clubs she kept seeing signs for as she drove down the freeway. Was he a Pink Lady Club type? Maybe he preferred Cock/Tails. Or maybe he went in for the sophisticated stylings of Bare Essence. The options were limitless.

But time wasn't. She looked at the clock. It was 10:47 a.m., less than forty-five minutes until she and Ryan were supposed to brief the Vegas FBI agents and hand over the case to them. She doubted she'd even get back to the station before they arrived. And the way things were going, she had no reason to argue that they should keep it. This whole trip had been a waste of time.

CHAPTER TWENTY TWO

Hannah sat on the floor of the basement, staring at the dead body of Robert Wilford Rylance.

For reasons she didn't understand, Bolton Crutchfield had left the man's body in the room with her. The two of them had shared the space all night and this morning too. Bolton had unchained her so she could at least move about. But because she didn't want to get close to the body, half of the space was essentially unusable for her.

The blood from his stab wounds, after initially spewing everywhere, had formed a large puddle, now mostly congealed, at the base of the stairs, making even the prospect of trying to climb them to escape unthinkable. Even though she's heard Bolton drive off earlier, she was sure that he would have prepared for that possibility.

She looked back over at Rylance and wondered if what Bolton had said about him was true. Was he really a pedophile or was that just some made up story to make her consider his murder somehow acceptable? And why did Bolton want her to kill him? It was like he was playing games with her, testing her, doing some weird mental experiment with her as the subject.

Another question circled her brain, one she tried to push away, which only made its pull stronger. What was this secret that Bolton kept promising to tell her, the one he hinted would change everything for her? What secret could have that kind of impact? He had said it was *her* secret. What did that mean? Was there even a secret at all or was that also part of whatever game he was playing?

Hannah physically shook her head, trying to force the thought out. She felt an anger rising in her, resentment at being manipulated. She was getting tired of being the victim. She'd been helpless when her foster parents were murdered.

She was tied up while her adoptive parents had been tortured and murdered. She watched as the same thing was almost done to that Jessie Hunt woman.

Suddenly, something stirred in her memory. It took a moment for her to recognize it. When she finally did, she realized it was pride. She was proud of how she had helped Hunt fight back against Xander Thurman. Even though her role had been small, there was something affirming about taking an active part in saving her own life. She wanted that feeling back.

There had to be a way to get it. There had to be something she could do to improve her chances of survival. Every moment that she was trapped down here increased the likelihood that she might never get out. If she wanted to see the light again from anything other than the tiny window in the corner, she needed to set aside her fears and take charge of her destiny.

How do I do that?

Instinctually, she knew the answer. Somehow she sensed that Bolton had left Rylance's body down here to toy with her. He wanted her to beg him to remove it, to be dependent on him. But if she could master her fear, then she wouldn't need to beg for anything.

So, despite the thumping of her heart in her chest, she walked over to the slumped, broken body of Robert Rylance, sitting forlornly tied to an old wooden chair, lifted her leg, and kicked him in the chest. Rylance teetered back in the chair, pausing briefly in midair, before collapsing back onto the floor.

His body landed hard. Then she heard another, smaller, more familiar thump. She recognized it immediately. It was the sound of a phone hitting the ground.

Hannah dashed over to find it. After several seconds, she saw it lying in the corner. She picked it up and hit the home button. Nothing happened.

Is it dead?

She pushed the button on the side and, after three seconds that felt like forever, it turned on. She immediately tried to call 911, but it didn't go through. She looked at the screen and noticed the words "no signal" in the corner. The basement walls must be interfering with it. She looked at the pool of blood at the base of the stairs again.

Screw it.

She hurried over and leapt onto the first step, then scurried up until she got to the second to last step near the door. She decided not to go any higher for fear of booby traps. She looked at the phone again. Still, it said "no signal."

She punched multiple buttons and got a message saying the phone needed face recognition to open. Then an alert popped up: 3% battery remaining.

Think, Hannah, think.

She forced herself to slow her breathing. She could do this. She'd done it before, with Jessie Hunt. She could survive this.

An idea shot into her head. Quickly, she darted back down the stairs. She tried to leap over the pooled blood. But this time she landed short and her right foot splashed in the liquid. She slipped and landed face down in the muck.

She gasped as she wrenched herself upward, trying not to breathe in the rust-scented substance. Then she heard it—the hum of an engine as Bolton returned.

Dammit!

Hannah got up. She knew from experience that the first thing Bolton always did upon returning from an errand was come down to check on her. That meant she had a minute, maybe ninety seconds to make this work.

She scrambled over to Rylance and held the phone to his face. It worked. The phone unlocked, his screen brightened, and all his apps appeared. She scrolled quickly through them until she found the one she hoped, prayed, he had. There it was: LinkedIn. All old people used it these days.

She clicked on the app and it opened up. Quickly she searched for a name: Jessie Hunt. There were a half dozen but only two were female. And only one, the account without a photo, listed the person's title as Criminal Forensic Profiler, Los Angeles Police Department. That was her.

Hannah thought for a second, then typed in a message as quickly as she could, ignoring the blood that smeared the screen as she moved her fingers. She was briefly interrupted by an alert that read: 2% battery remaining.

She was almost done when she heard the front door of the house creak open. She finished, reviewed the words one last time, and hit send. She wasn't surprised when she got a notification that the message could not be sent due to lack of a signal.

She quickly wiped the phone screen on a clean portion of her pants and shoved it back in Rylance's pocket. The door to the basement opened and she darted back the center of the room, where she stood, hugging the pole.

"I'll have your lunch in a few minutes, Miss Hann..."

Bolton Crutchfield, who had been easing his way down the stairs, stopped cold at the sight below him. Hannah, covered in blood, clutching the wooden pole in the center of the room; Rylance, still in the chair but lying on his back; the pool of blood at the bottom of the stairs, now a Jackson Pollock painting.

"What happened here?' he asked slowly.

Hannah launched in, hoping her legitimate anxiety would play as hysteria.

"I just couldn't stand it anymore. I felt like he was staring at me so I knocked him over. But I slipped in the blood. I think it was like his way of getting back at me. Please, just take him out of here. Please!"

Bolton smiled sympathetically.

"If I do that, what will you do for me?"

"What do you want?" she demanded suspiciously.

"Nothing like that," he assured her. "I only want for you to let me tell you your secret and for you to really hear it and understand what it means. Are you willing to do that, Miss Hannah?"

"Yes. That's fine. Please, just take him out of here."

"As you wish, Miss Hannah. Please stand back against the far wall."

Hannah did as she was told and watched with genuine nervousness as Bolton slowly dragged Robert Rylance's body up the stairs. With each thump as he bumped on a wooden stair, Hannah silently pleaded with the phone gods.

Let that battery last.

CHAPTER TWENTY THREE

I t didn't make any sense.

Jessie listened as Ryan reviewed the Vegas doctor's murder file while she drove back to the station. But no matter how many details he offered, Jessie couldn't understand why Lexi was committing these crimes. It felt like there was a piece missing, one that, if she could locate it, would make the whole puzzle fit together.

"There are no other cases in Las Vegas that fit the profile, with a john drugged and robbed, even if he wasn't murdered?"

She knew she had asked that before and that Ryan had already answered the question.

"No," he said, impressively managing not to sound irked.

"I'm sorry to keep coming back to that. But I just don't buy that her first try at this sort of thing was a perfectly executed murder plan in a fancy Las Vegas hotel. The first time is almost always messier than that."

"Vegas PD went back two years, Jessie," he said. "There wasn't a single case of a drugging and robbery in that time that matched this one. Of course, that doesn't mean someone just didn't report it. I could easily see some guy waking up naked and without his wallet and deciding it wasn't worth it to say anything. Maybe he figured he didn't want to risk surviving the robbery just to be killed by his wife later."

Something about the comment stirred an idea in Jessie. She let it percolate for a moment.

"Jessie?" Ryan said. "Still there?"

"Yeah," she answered, realizing she'd gone completely silent. "I just thought of something. What if we're looking for the wrong thing? Despite the organization and planning, these murders feel like acts of anger, vengeance even. Maybe we shouldn't be looking for druggings and robberies of johns that didn't end in death. Maybe we should be looking for murders of johns that didn't involve drugging."

Jessie waited for a response, unsure whether Ryan would consider her theory crazy. After a few seconds, she got her answer.

"Pulling up the Vegas database now," he said. "Give me a second to put in the new parameters."

While he did, Jessie tried to picture how a "first murder" would take place. She suspected it might not start out as a murder at all. Maybe it was a date that got out of control. Maybe the john wanted too much or pushed too hard and she just lost it.

"I've gone back three years," Ryan said, interrupting her thoughts. "I find four confirmed dead johns that were definitively ruled homicides."

"How did they die?"

"Three were shot. One was pushed out a window by a woman claiming she was fighting off a rape attempt."

"I don't think Lexi is a shooting type of gal," Jessie said. "What happened to the window woman?"

"She's . . . oh, never mind. She's currently serving three to five at the Florence McClure Women's Correctional Center."

"Okay," Jessie said, rethinking on the fly. "What about unsolved murders of married or single men generally, not necessarily johns specifically, not using a gun, found in a hotel?"

She could hear Ryan typing furiously.

"I've got nothing," he said, dejected.

They were both quiet for several seconds.

Don't make assumptions. Let the evidence be your guide.

That was the primary advice given to her by the behavioral science experts when she'd attended the FBI Academy. And yet, Jessie couldn't shake the feeling that she was still making some big ones.

"Hey, Ryan," she said, a new thought forming at the corner of her mind, "can you redo the last query but remove the hotel filter?'

"Doing it now," he said.

"Anything?" she asked anxiously.

"A few," he replied. "I'm scrolling through them now. Okay, there were six unsolved murders of single or married men not using guns in Clark County in the last three years."

"How many of those took place in a home or apartment?"

"Two," he said a few seconds later.

"Can you describe them?"

Okay," he said. "The first was last year in an apartment building. It was a stabbing of a young male. No one was ever convicted but during the course of the investigation, at least four people were arrested."

"How did that happen?"

"It looks like the building was abandoned. It was a notorious drug den. The guy who was stabbed was an addict, as were all the suspects."

Jessie shook her head. That didn't sound right.

"What about the other murder?"

"That was four months ago," Ryan said. "Also a single male, thirty years old; killed in his own home in Henderson, a suburb of Vegas. He was bludgeoned to death."

"Whoa!"

"Yeah. The photos are pretty brutal. He was found…Jessie, he was found completely naked in his own washing machine. They think he was beaten with a baseball bat but one was never found. They searched the entire house for prints but never found any that matched a legitimate suspect. Also, the whole house had been wiped down. And the guy's body had been scrubbed with disinfectant."

"This sounds like our girl," Jessie said, a little embarrassed by the excitement in her voice.

"It sure does," Ryan agreed, matching her enthusiasm but without the guilt.

How long do we have before we have to brief those FBI guys?" she asked.

"About ten minutes. Why?"

"Because we need Decker to stall them. You think he'd do that?"

"Depends," he replied. "What reason can I give him?"

"Tell him I have an idea."

Chapter Twenty Four

The FBI agents were pissed.

Jessie could tell before they even said a word. One, a tall, muscular African-American man in a perfectly tailored suit, was pacing back and forth in the mirrored conference room. The other, a squat, barrel-chested white guy with an unflattering crewcut, sat very still, clearly seething.

She couldn't blame them. The meeting was supposed to start at 11:30 but she didn't even get back until fifteen minutes after that. Meanwhile, Decker told them she'd been stuck in traffic (mostly true) and wouldn't be back until noon (not true at all).

By the time he walked in with Jessie and Ryan, the agents looked like they were ready to pull out their guns.

"I am *so* sorry," she said before either of them could get a word out, channeling her inner ditz. "I was following up a lead out in Redlands and it turned out to be an epic fail. And traffic on the way back was unreal. I'm sure you guys understand. It must have been brutal coming in all the way from Vegas. What is that, four hours?"

"Actually, five," the pacing agent said. "But we allowed ourselves extra time to get here because we had a scheduled meeting and we try to be respectful of other people's time."

"Totally legitimate critique," she agreed. "Won't happen again, I swear. I'm Jessie Hunt, by the way. This is Detective Ryan Hernandez. I understand you already met Captain Decker."

The pacing agent stared at her for a moment, then seemed to decide he'd dressed her down enough for the moment.

"I'm Special Agent Moseley," he said and then nodded at the seething agent. "That's Special Agent Peretti. Shall we get started?"

"Absolutely," Ryan said, sitting down and putting a manila file and a laptop on the table. Everyone else sat as well, joining the still seething and still silent Peretti.

"Your captain told us you might have some new information on a possible suspect," Mosely said. "I was surprised to hear that. The last update from yesterday was that there were no possibles."

"You know how it is," Jessie said perkily. "Sometimes a good night's sleep changes everything. Am I right?"

Neither agent spoke and Decker shot her a warning glare. Out of the corner of her eye, she could see Ryan trying not to smile.

"Shall I proceed?" she asked.

"Who is it?" Peretti nearly spat.

"I'm sorry?"

"You've wasted enough of our time," he growled. "You say you have a possible suspect. Who is it?"

Jessie sighed deeply and offered an apologetic smile.

"I don't actually know just yet. But we're working on it."

"I'm confused," Mosely said. "Do you or do you not have a possible suspect?"

"We do," she assured him. "But we don't know who she is."

Peretti turned to Mosely with a disgusted look on his face.

"I can't believe we came all the way to this smog-choked city to put up with this crap."

"Actually," Jessie submitted, "the smog was much worse in the 1970s. It's really improved, although the summers can be bad."

"Ms. Hunt," Captain Decker said slowly. "Maybe now would be a good time to walk the agents through your scenario. That might help move things along and prevent anyone from having a coronary."

Jessie gave him a sweet smile.

"Of course, Captain." She turned to the agents. "Apologies again, gentlemen. If you would give me just two minutes of your attention, we can walk you through what we have. Sound okay?"

"We're all ears," Mosely said. Jessie admired his restraint, considering all her intentionally provocative button-pushing.

"Okay, here we go," she said, grabbing the manila file and pulling out four sheets of paper. "Here are our four victims so far."

"Four?" Peretti interrupted. "I thought we only had three—the two here and the one in Vegas. Was there another murder last night?"

"Agent Peretti," Jessie said, "if you would allow me to proceed, I promise I'll make everything clear in due course."

She got another scowl from him but he said nothing more. She continued.

"To our knowledge, there have been two murders in Los Angeles. We know of a third in Las Vegas, Dr. Harvey Kostner. But we believe our suspect committed a fourth murder, her first one, in Las Vegas four months ago. That victim was named Daniel Beane."

"He doesn't sound familiar," Mosely said.

"There's no reason he should," Jessie assured him. "He didn't fit the original profile. Beane was a thirty-year-old banker who worked in downtown Las Vegas but lived in Henderson in a single-family home. He was unmarried and, other than one arrest for being drunk and disorderly in college, he has no record."

"But," Ryan picked up from there, "he does have a record of frequenting bars and casinos in the Fremont Street district, an area I'm sure you gentlemen know far better than we do. His personal banking records also often show withdrawals in the three to five hundred range at ATMs in many of those hotels. One might think that was for gambling purposes. But in almost every case, after getting the money, he made no more digital transactions that night."

"So you're saying he got the money for whores and left the hotels with them right after withdrawing the cash?" Peretti said impatiently.

"Correct," Jessie said. "That seems to be exactly what he did on the night of November eighth. Unfortunately, his date that night didn't go so well for him. His body was found in his home the following Tuesday, naked and beaten so badly that his face wasn't recognizable."

"Was he drugged?" Mosely asked.

"No," Jessie said.

"No drugging. No hotel. What makes you think this is the same killer?" he asked, more curious than challenging.

"It was a hunch at first. I suspected this might be Lexi's first murder. I think it was unplanned and therefore sloppy. But it has some of the same hallmarks as the others, notably the victim being found naked, as well as cleaning the crime scene and the victim's body to ensure there was no biological evidence to go on."

"Why do you think it was unplanned?" Peretti asked, no longer looking so peeved.

"LVPD found scratches and indentations in the bed posts. Their CSU discovered material in the scratches consistent with handcuffs, bedsheets, scarves, and other items that might have been used to tie someone down."

Peretti asked the obvious question.

"You think he wanted a little rough play, that it got too rough, and she made him pay for it?"

"Something like that," Jessie confirmed.

"I feel like you're holding back, Ms. Hunt," Mosely said. "Is there more?"

"There is," she said. "We checked Beane's calls in the twenty-four hours prior to his death and compared them to the call log on Dr. Kostner's final day alive. No numbers matched. But both received calls from burner phones within that time window. Each phone was purchased with cash—no surprise there. But using the numbers, we were able to trace the location where each phone was bought. Turns out it was the same convenience store."

"Were you able to get surveillance footage?" Peretti asked, now beginning to look excited.

Ryan opened the laptop, faced the screen toward the agents, and hit "play." They all watched as a grainy video showed a woman with long blonde hair buying a phone, a bag of chips, and a soda. Then it skipped to a second video. In that one, a woman wearing what was obviously intended as a disguise—a bulky coat, a baseball cap, and sunglasses, with her blonde hair tied in a bun—purchased only a burner phone and walked out. As they watched the footage, Jessie felt her cell phone, which she'd put on "silent," buzz in her pocket.

"Before you ask," Ryan said, "our tech folks did some facial recognition and determined that it's the same woman in both videos."

"Is there any exterior footage that shows her getting in a car?" Mosely asked.

"No," Jessie admitted. "She walked away from the store in both cases. There are too many gaps in camera placement near there to follow her after that. But we did notice something else."

She hit "play" again. The footage was clearly from her first visit to the store, when her hair was down. But this was before she bought the phone. She walked around the store, looking at snacks and eventually picking up the chips they'd seen her with in the previous footage. Then she opened the door to the soda fridge.

"Can we get prints from that?" Peretti asked.

"I'm afraid not," Jessie answered. "Hundreds of people touch that door every week. Besides, according to the manager, they wipe those door handles down every night and this was months ago. But they don't wipe *everything* down."

As she said that, Lexi glanced at a sunglasses rack near the soda fridge. She spun it around until she saw a golden, star-framed pair at the top of the display. She reached up to grab them and put them on, studying herself in the tiny mirror. Apparently unsatisfied, she returned them to their slot, gripping the glasses by their lenses.

"She got her prints all over them," Mosely said quietly.

"Yes she did," Jessie agreed.

"Any chance those glasses are still there?" he asked, sounding cautiously hopeful.

"They were there," Jessie said. "That is, until an LVPD crime scene unit went by at our request earlier this morning to collect them for analysis. They're hard at work right now and I imagine that we may be able to give you gentlemen a definitive ID on her in the very near future."

"Do they have a timetable?" Peretti wanted to know.

"I asked them to call as soon as they knew something," she said, pushing her chair back from the table and standing up. "I'm afraid that's all we have for now, gentlemen. In the meantime, we have a wonderful array of pastries in the kitchen, if you want to avail yourself of them."

"I could go for a scone," Peretti said, suddenly almost friendly.

"I thought you were gluten free now," Mosely protested.

"Only in Vegas. On the road, that rule is more of a suggestion."

"Does your wife know that?" Mosely asked.

"We're going to let you guys work this one out on your own," Jessie said with a broad smile. "But we should reconvene once Vegas CSU reaches out. Sound good?"

The agents nodded and headed for the kitchen.

"Good work," Decker said as he headed back to his office. "Keep me apprised."

"Yes sir," Jessie said.

Ryan started to follow him out but Jessie shook her head almost impercep-
tibly and he held back.

"What is it?"

"I got a call while we were talking," she said. "I think we're going to want
to listen to it somewhere private."

CHAPTER TWENTY FIVE

Jessie hadn't lied, at least not technically.

When she said that the LVPD techs were hard at work, that statement was true. And she did ask them to call when they had something. It's just that she had asked them to call Camille Guadino, the rookie crime scene tech, rather than reach out to her directly. Then Guadino would fill her in on the details.

So, officially at least, LVPD still hadn't called Jessie and therefore, she had no obligation to share anything with the FBI agents just yet. She was dancing on the head of the world's tiniest pin, but it was at least nominally defensible.

They only dared listen to the message when they were alone in the observation section of a currently unused interrogation room. Guadino gave them the name of the person whose prints were on those sunglass lenses. Jessie wrote it down and, as casually as possible, they returned to their desks, where they plugged her name into the system. Jessie tried to keep her expression neutral as information filled the screen.

What she saw there thrilled and horrified her at the same time. The prints belonged to Alexis Cutter, an eighteen-year-old from Las Vegas who'd gone missing over a year ago after running away from her home following an incident with her stepfather.

"Alexis," she heard Ryan mutter before looking over at her. "Lexi."

Jessie nodded and looked back at the screen, on which the photo of a girl from her high school student ID stared back at her. It was the same girl from the hotel footage. She wasn't as made up in the ID photo. But she had the same long blonde hair, perfectly sculpted features, and stunning, sky-blue eyes that seemed to pierce the soul of whoever she looked at.

Jessie reviewed her records, scanning quickly while looking up intermittently to make sure Agents Mosely and Peretti weren't around.

Alexis Cutter, or "Alex" as police interviews with her friends said she preferred, was the only daughter of Marlene Thomason, who had divorced her father when Alex was four. It had been just the two of them until Marlene married Steve Kupisch, a thirty-four-year-old twice-married electrician who had served time for statutory rape when he was in his twenties.

Soon after the marriage, Alex's grades fell off a cliff. She quit the volleyball team and Mathletes, and was disciplined repeatedly for tardiness and absences. Then one night when she was seventeen and while her mother was working the night shift at a diner, an ambulance was called to the house.

Steve had been stabbed and Alex was nowhere to be found. Her fingerprints were on the knife. His friends, who had been hanging out with him that night, all claimed that Alex had attacked him, unprovoked, in what seemed like a drug-fueled frenzy.

Even without Kupisch's personal history, Jessie would have been skeptical. Despite the general agreement among his friends that Steve wasn't at fault and that Alex attacked him for no reason, all the men were extremely drunk and the particulars of their stories varied wildly.

Furthermore, there were no defensive wounds on Steve, which suggested that he was the aggressor. Alex's bedroom door was broken and her room was covered in his blood, which indicated the altercation had happened there, despite all assertions to the contrary. In addition, Alexis's dog, Lola, was found dead, with a broken neck. Kupisch said it had attacked him for no reason and he had to kill her in self-defense. That claim seemed dubious as well.

But in the end, there wasn't enough evidence to charge anyone and Alex disappearing made it impossible to confirm or rebut Steve's story. The case languished. Eight months later, just weeks after Marlene divorced him, Kupisch was arrested for sexually assaulting an underage girl in a public park. He was currently in county jail awaiting trial.

As for Alex, her trail dried up that night. There was no record of her going to a hospital. She never reached out to any friends. She never made any purchases with the one credit card her mother had given her. It was like she simply dropped off the face of the earth.

Jessie tried to imagine what life must have been like for Alexis Cutter, how bad it must have been for her in those two years before she finally fought back. How many times must her stepfather have abused her? Was there any real chance her mother didn't know the truth, even with her daughter changing, seemingly overnight, from a promising student-athlete into a borderline juvenile delinquent? How betrayed must she have felt? How angry?

Jessie pictured the girl going into one of the few industries in which she could make money without having to meet paperwork requirements: the sex trade. With her stunning looks and precocious body, she would have likely garnered interest from anyone looking for that sort of thing. But even if she could be somewhat selective about her clients, she couldn't predict how they'd behave behind closed doors. She surely endured untold indignities in the service of survival.

And then, one crisp November evening, she must have hit her limit. Maybe Daniel Beane made her do something her stepfather had. Maybe he made her do something she'd done a hundred times before. Maybe he threatened her life. Whatever he did, it was clearly the last straw. The remnants of Daniel Beane's spongy, butchered face were proof of that.

How must that have felt, after so many years without any power, to finally be the one in control? Surely it was a rush to get payback against someone who'd treated her like an object to be used. It was almost certainly a feeling she'd want to recreate.

And since her job repeatedly put her in a position where she had to attend to the basest desires of men who had no respect for her, it must have been a constant itch, one that she eventually decided to scratch again with Dr. Harvey Kostner.

Only this time she was prepared. This time she planned it out. Had she gotten the sedative from Kostner, a doctor with a reputation as a drunk, and one who had been accused of selling prescriptions, though he was never formally charged? It seemed plausible.

And once her plan worked with him, it made sense that she would leave town. It was simply too risky to stay in a city where she might bump into someone she knew. Everyone assumed Alexis Cutter was dead. If they learned otherwise, people might start asking questions. And her burgeoning obsession depended on being the kind of person no one asked questions about.

So she must have fled to Los Angeles, where she kept a low profile for several months, figuring out how the city's sex business worked and where she could fit in without rocking the boat. Apparently she determined that the downtown scene best met her needs.

So very recently, as she was a new face to local bartenders, she would have started working the local upscale hotels. And after a stretch during which she'd managed to hold out on feeding her thirst for vengeance, she had picked up where she left off in Las Vegas.

She was punishing the kinds of men who had hurt and abused her. All of them were powerful men who didn't care about the people they used: a slimy banker, a shady doctor, a corrupt politician, a lecherous agent—all of them users, all potential abusers.

Of course there was one supposed victim who didn't fit the profile—the computer programmer from Redlands. He was none of those things, at least not on the surface. Jessie started to ponder how he might be connected when another idea invaded her thoughts.

"She's not going to stop," she said, more to herself than Ryan.

"What?" he asked.

"Alexis is a planner. But last night was much more slapdash than her first LA kill. Unlike with Gordon Maines, she murdered the agent in the same hotel where she met him. I think she's losing her ability to be methodical and patient. She's developing a tolerance for the high she gets from the kills because it'll never be enough. As long as her stepfather still haunts her, she'll never be able to stop. Each new kill is an opportunity to punish him by proxy, to make him suffer through their torment."

"Okay," Ryan said. "So what does that mean? That she's going after her stepfather next? You think she's gone back to Vegas?"

"She can't. He's in jail awaiting trial. I guarantee you she knows that. Otherwise I'm sure she would have gone after him by now. It must be infuriating that he's out of her grasp. I think that's why this is escalating. She's pouring her fury into these other men. And no amount of strangling is going to fill the emptiness she feels. She's not going to stop until she's caught or killed. And I'm worried about something else too."

"Like that's not enough?" Ryan said. "What else could there be?"

"I'm worried that she's so far gone now, she won't just try to hunt down some scumbag. She might just pick the first guy she can find, no matter how innocent he is."

Chapter Twenty Six

A lex loved Hollywood.

Something about the old-world glamour of the town appealed to her, even if it was sometimes hard to find it these days amid all the multiplexes and strip malls.

She loved having dates take her to places like Musso & Frank Grill, the 100-year-old steakhouse where the waiters still wore tuxedos; or the Magic Castle, the slightly cheesy but still enthralling Hollywood Hills establishment that only allowed entry (through a hidden door) to professional magician club members and their guests. She was a sucker for all of it, especially the stuff that reminded her of those classic black-and-white movies. It was nothing like the permanent neon glow that lit the Vegas nightscape.

That's why she was so excited that the next Reckoning, her final one in Los Angeles, would take place here at the Hollywood Roosevelt Hotel. It was only eight miles away from downtown, but it was a universe away from the sleek, modern towers that dotted the skyline.

The legend was that the ghost of Montgomery Clift haunted a room on the ninth floor. She was tempted to ask her next mark to request it specifically. But it was almost certainly already booked. Besides, that kind of request draws attention, which makes people like front desk clerks remember the requester. That was counterproductive.

She sat at the bar, Teddy's, and, as was her habit, gave herself a quick once-over in the closest mirror. Everything was in place. Her blue cocktail dress not only matched her eyes, it popped nicely against her flowing red hair. Her creamy silk scarf covered her shoulders against the surprising chill in the air. She settled in. It was 9:06 p.m.—prime hunting time. Her prey would be arriving soon.

Jessie was starting to doubt herself.

They'd been at it for hours. It was after nine and still nothing. Not a single hit at any of the apartment buildings or hotels they'd checked.

She'd been sure that Alex would have set up home base at a cheap place in the downtown area, one that was within walking distance of most of the hotels she frequented. But it also had to accept cash and not require ID, which would be priorities for a woman trying to stay off the grid.

Unfortunately, it became clear after about an hour of making calls that no one who ran these places was going to volunteer that they operated that way. This had to be an in-person undertaking. So Ryan and Jessie, along with four uniformed officers, were canvassing the neighborhood, visiting every shady residential option within the general vicinity of the hotels Alex had visited.

Jessie, after some prodding from Ryan, had even reluctantly relented and agreed to tell Agents Mosely and Peretti about Alex's identity so they could enlist the bureau's resources. Her concern that they would bungle the case and let Alex escape was outweighed by the realization that they needed all the help they could get. Still, she told the uniformed officers that if they uncovered anything suspicious, to contact her or Ryan on a private channel.

Around 9:15, just as Jessie felt a blister pop on her throbbing left pinkie toe, they got a call. Officer Beatty, getting a break from condo security duty, was at the Central Arms, a weekly hotel just off Pershing Square, only blocks from the Biltmore Hotel where Alex had met up with Gordon Maines. According to him, the night manager was being "especially squirrelly" in answering questions.

"We'll be there in two minutes," Ryan said.

It actually took closer to six because Jessie was limping slowly on her swollen, hobbled feet. When they arrived at the Central Arms, a narrow, shabby building squished between a warehouse and an Army surplus store, Jessie felt a glimmer of hope. This was exactly the kind of easy-to-miss, hard-to-like place that someone looking for anonymity might embrace.

They walked in, where Officer Beatty was sitting exhaustedly on a wooden bench across from the bulletproof vestibule where the manager stood defiantly. He was a swarthy man of indeterminate ethnicity. In his late thirties, with a bushy shock of blackish-gray hair and an equally unkempt beard, he looked ready for a showdown.

"What's the story, Beatty?" Ryan asked the officer.

"He was chatty at first, all 'how can I help you, officer.' Then I showed him the photo of the girl and he clammed up. He didn't definitively deny seeing her but suddenly his memory is all hazy. Won't let me look at his hotel register. Won't show me receipts. Nothing. All the other managers were a challenge. But he's the first one to act this way."

"Okay, good work," Ryan said. "Join us at the window in case what he tells us changes from his story to you."

They all approached the manager's window. Jessie noticed him put his hands on the counter and press down hard. His face was set in insolence.

"This is police harassment!" he shouted in a thick but understandable accent before anyone said a word to him. "I will sue!"

Ryan looked at Jessie.

"Preference?" he asked.

Jessie looked back at the man. Though she didn't know his background, she sensed that the best approach was to get him out of his defensive, self-righteous crouch. That meant making him feel he'd violated even his own moral code.

"I go first," she muttered under his breath. "When he's dismissive and con-descending, you take over and send him into a shame spiral."

"Sounds fun," Ryan said, genuinely enthused by the prospect.

"You have a weird way of having fun, Hernandez," she said.

"And you're definitely the first person who's ever told me that," he replied snarkily. "Why don't you get started? The clock is ticking."

He was right. If Jessie's theory was correct, Alex might very well strike again tonight. And they were currently right in the window of time when she seemed to hook her targets. She turned to the manager and gave him her biggest smile.

"Good evening sir," she said, pretending he hadn't just made shouted threats to sue. "I'm Jessie Hunt with the Los Angeles Police Department. What's your name?"

"Omar," he said as if it was an epithet.

"Omar, it's great to meet you. I hope you're having a pleasant evening."

"Not with him around," he said, pointing at Officer Beatty.

"Right. Well, not everybody can be best friends, I guess. But maybe we can find our way there. I understand that Officer Beatty showed you a photo of a young woman a little earlier. Is that correct?"

"I already told him. I don't remember if I saw her. I see many people every day."

"And I get that. You must be very busy, Omar. But surely you'd remember if someone was staying at your hotel, especially if they'd been here for more than just a night or two. If you're good at your job, you'd have to, right?"

"What can I say?" Omar replied, shrugging. "I'm getting older. Memory's not so great anymore."

"Sure," Jessie said, leaning up close and resting her elbows on the counter. "I get it. The same thing happens to me. But you saw the photo of that girl. She's not just some random tourist. She's beautiful. No healthy, virile man would forget a woman who looked like that. And yet, you can't recall her?"

"Are you insulting me?" he demanded, his voice not yet a shout but heading in that direction.

"I would never do that, Omar," she said, sounding scandalized. "I just can't believe a man of your age would forget about a woman who looked like that. Maybe you aren't . . . interested in attractive women."

She let the suggestion hang in there, certain he'd draw the conclusion she was hinting at.

"You *are* insulting me," he accused, his voice echoing through the hallway. "You come in here and say that I don't like women. You say I am a gay!"

"I would never, Omar . . ." she started before he cut her off.

"Don't talk to me. You are a disgrace. You are like a mangy dog!"

Jessie didn't reply. Instead she clutched her hand to her chest as if she'd been cut to the quick. Ryan stepped forward, dramatically pulling her aside.

"What did you say?" he growled.

"You heard her," Omar yelled back, though not quite as loudly as before. "She says I am not a man. It's a disgrace."

"You just insulted a woman, Omar," he said loudly, squaring up. "But not just any woman—she is the law. And she's my fiancée too! She was only asking you questions and you called her a dog. I don't care about the picture anymore. I'm going to handle this man to man. Officer Beatty, take Ms. Hunt outside. Don't come back in, no matter what you hear. You got it?"

"Yes sir," Beatty said crisply, picking up on his role in the plan.

Omar's face had gone from to defiant to terrified in a matter of seconds.

"Wait," he said. "I didn't know she was yours. How could I?"

Ryan continued talking to Beatty, pretending not to hear Omar's words.

"Call for an ambulance in five minutes, but not before. Understand?"

"Yes, sir!" Beatty said, looking like he might actually salute. "Please come with me, Ms. Hunt."

Jessie stepped toward him, trying to appear as crestfallen as possible, even wiping away an invisible tear with her sleeve.

"Wait, this isn't needed," Omar pleaded from behind her. "I remember her. I do. I can show you her room."

"I don't give a damn about that now," Ryan snarled. "You come out from behind that window or I'll drag you out myself."

"Wait," Omar screeched, now in full-on beg mode. "Let me take you to her room. I'll show you now."

Jessie turned around to see Ryan staring Omar down.

"Now," he said to the man quietly.

Omar fumbled for his keys and opened the door to the vestibule.

"This way," he said, scurrying in front of them. "And I am sorry. I was just doing my job to protect the guests here, to protect their privacy. I meant no harm."

"Omar," Ryan said, winking at Jessie when he was sure the manager was looking the other way. "Just shut up."

Omar didn't say another word.

CHAPTER TWENTY SEVEN

A lex could tell he was the guy the second he walked in the bar.
She watched him in the mirror. The short, squat balding man in the fancy suit started looking around as soon as he stepped through the door. When he saw her, his eyes got that shark-like look she was so used to and he immediately came over.

"Red hair, blue dress, silk scarf—nice ensemble," he said, not even making a pretense of introducing himself.

"Thanks," she said, efficiently hiding the distaste she almost immediately felt toward him.

He gave off a brusque, entitled vibe that she suspected he took with him everywhere. In real life, she would avoid a man like this like the plague. But tonight, he was exactly what she was after.

"I'm Barry," he said, sitting down on the barstool beside her without extending his hand. "What do you call yourself?"

"Nice to meet you, Barry. I'm Lexi."

"Lexi," he repeated. "You look lonely here all by yourself."

"Oh, I'm not lonely," she assured him. "Just alone. But I'm happy to have company if he's a good conversationalist."

"Lexi. I've got to be honest. I'm not in a very chatty mood tonight. I'm interested in a more . . . physical interaction."

He wasn't even attempting to play the game. This job was never a self-esteem boost but Barry had a special gift for rubbing it in. Alex felt like a slab of meat the guy was pointing out to the butcher at the grocery store.

"Wow, you're a real charmer, Barry," she said, deciding to rein him in a little. "What do you do?"

She could feel her pulse quickening at the possibility of taking down another asshole. But she had to be cautious. She had to be sure he wasn't a cop. More important, she had to be sure he would be a satisfying candidate.

"Oh, I get it. You need a little warming up. Okay, I'm an executive with a film studio. I make the crappy movies you overpay to see. How's that for conversation?"

I'm going to love taking you down.

"It's great, Barry. That sounds really fascinating. Thanks for humoring me."

"You bet," he said, shifting on his stool. "So what's it going to take for you to humor *me?*"

Alex stared at him. She wasn't going to take any chances.

"You know, Barry, I hear this hotel has eight floors. Is that true?"

For a second, he looked at her like she was crazy. The hotel had twelve floors. Then he seemed to get it.

"I don't think that's right," he finally replied. "I heard it was more like four floors."

She didn't love his attempt to haggle. Despite how deserving of a takedown he appeared to be, Barry increasingly seemed like more trouble than he was worth.

"No, I'm pretty positive it's eight floors. A gorgeous hotel like this, so wonderfully decorated and such a pedigree, four floors seems like, well, not nearly enough."

Barry looked her over greedily and seemed to reconsider.

"Why don't you get yourself a drink while you ponder?" she suggested.

"I don't drink, actually," he said. "I like to keep my edge when I'm dealing with all my soused and coked up industry counterparts. But I might be willing to concede that this place has six floors."

Alex glanced over at him casually. But beneath her unhurried demeanor, she did a quick calculation.

Combative. Not so taken with me that he won't wrangle over cost. Doesn't drink.

Despite all her instincts screaming that this jerk deserved to be ended, she had to move on. It was simply too risky. If he didn't drink, she doubted she could easily drug him. Lorazepam had a bitter taste that was detectable in water but far less so in alcohol. And even though he was an out of shape troll, she couldn't risk trying to take him out if he was alert.

"You know, Barry?" she said, her voice icy as she turned away from him. "I just remembered, I'm meeting a gal pal and she should be here any minute. But it was nice talking to you."

"That's it?" he asked incredulously.

"That's it," she said, not even looking at him anymore.

"Bitch!" he hissed before turning and waddling away.

Every cell in her screamed that she should grab the ice pick lying on the bar, chase after him, and plunge it in the back of his skull. Instead, she sighed deeply through a forced smile as she re-crossed her legs.

Time to improvise.

She surveyed the room, trying not to look like she was prowling. At the far end of the bar were three guys who looked to be in their mid-twenties. Despite their ages, they all wore meticulously "informal" casual wear, including loosely tucked button-down shirts and tailored jeans.

She dismissed them as potential victims—too young, clearly not established enough to pay her fee. But just as she looked away, she noticed that one of the guys—the least put-together of them—kept giving her awkward, darting glances, trying not to be noticed.

She smiled at him, despite herself. He obviously wasn't a contender for the Reckoning, but with his curly brown hair, wire-rimmed glasses, and lanky, baby-giraffe-like frame, he was adorable in a gawky, self-conscious way. Knowing there was no consequence to it, she winked at him.

His buddies saw it and whispered something to him that she imagined was along the lines of "go for it, dude!" And to her surprise and mild admiration, he got up, adjusted his glasses, and loped in her direction.

This is a mistake. Don't waste your time. Find a legitimate candidate.

But then he was there, standing beside her. His curls bounced slightly and she realized it was because he was literally shaking.

"Hi, I'm Andy," he said, his voice dry. "Can I buy you a drink?"

"Hi, Andy. I'm Lexi. I already have a drink."

"Oh. Yeah. Sorry," he said and started to turn away.

"You give up that easy, Andy?' she asked, teasingly.

He turned back around, looking half-confused and half-hopeful.

"I guess not?" he asked more than said. "I just thought you were politely telling me to go away with the drink thing."

"No, Andy," she assured him. "I was just saying that I already have a drink. Maybe I should buy you one."

He smiled cautiously, seeming to rediscover his ungainly confidence.

"I already have a drink too," he said, holding up his glass. "But don't take that the wrong way. I'm not giving you the brush-off."

"Touché," she said, smiling again despite herself. "Look at you with the quips, Andy."

A goofy grin spread across his face, which he tried to force down.

"I'm very quippy," he told her with faux seriousness.

"Are you a stand-up comedian or something?"

"Oh no, nothing that exciting."

"A librarian then?" she kidded.

"Closer."

"You'll have to tell me, Andy. Otherwise I'll be guessing all night."

"I'm an app designer," he said sheepishly.

"Is that something to be embarrassed about?" she asked.

"No. It's just not that exciting."

"Let me be the judge of that. What's the app?"

"Okay. It's like a social calendar," he said, his demeanor getting instantly more comfortable. "It aggregates events from multiple sources and suggests them to the user based on their preferences."

"Clever. Should I have heard of it?"

"I don't know," he said. "We launched about six months ago. You seem like the target age range. But it depends how into nightlife and social media you are."

"Not very," she said.

"But you're out here in this bar tonight," he pointed out.

She gave him a sideways glance, not sure if he was being sincere or making fun of her.

"That's more of a work thing," she volunteered cautiously.

"Oh, yeah, I get it. You aspiring models and actress types have to mingle all the time, right?"

Lexi stared at him, dumbstruck for the first time in recent memory. Was it really possible that this guy didn't know what she was?

Andy saw her expression and, misinterpreting it as taking offense, tried to fix it.

"Oh, man. I'm sorry. That was rude. I shouldn't have just assumed you were a model or an actress. That was total stereotyping. You could be a chemical engineer. It's just—Hollywood, fancy bar, you looking like, no offense, but you're really attractive. I just figured you were in that business. I...I...I'm sorry."

She put her hand on top of his and, though he seemed startled, he didn't pull it away.

"It's okay, Andy. I don't take offense."

"Oh, okay, good. Thanks. Sorry again."

"You're forgiven."

"So what *do* you do, Lexi?"

"I'm an aspiring model," she said.

He stared at her for a second before trying to force down a giggle that turned into a loud guffaw. She started laughing too. She couldn't remember the last time she had really laughed.

"So," she said, moving the conversation away from herself. "Are you here because your app said this was the place to be tonight?"

He looked aghast.

"Oh god, no. I don't usually go out. I'm more of a homebody. In fact, I only live a few blocks from here but I've never actually been inside this hotel until tonight. My friends and I are here because we're celebrating. The app had its IPO today and it went really well. Like, really well."

"That's great," Alex said, not entirely sure what that meant though she got the distinct impression it was a big deal.

"Yeah, anyway, enough about all that. It's kind of boring. Have you ever been here before, Lexi?"

"No. But I was always curious. I heard there's a haunted room on the ninth floor."

"No way!" Andy said, awestruck. "That's totally awesome. We should check it out."

She was briefly tempted to agree before remembering how unwise it would be to ask.

"I'm sure the room is already booked," she said quickly. "Lots of people know about it."

"Oh," he said, disappointed. "Still, that's really cool. I love that kind of thing. Old Hollywood legends and stuff. Like the Magic Castle up the hill. Have you ever been?"

"No," she admitted, amazed at this guy who seemed to be her pop culture twin. "But I've always wanted to go."

"Oh, it's really wild. A magician guy I know is a member and he invited me one time. It's really fun. You kind of get swept away in it, you know?"

"Mmm-hmm."

He looked at her, suddenly nervous.

"I'm sure I could get him to hook me up again. We should go sometime . . . if you were interested."

He gulped hard and took a long swig of his drink. She could tell he was about to start shaking again. Against all her instincts, she heard her voice reply.

"Sure. That sounds fun."

His face broke out again into that childlike grin. He looked like a little boy opening his presents on Christmas morning.

Could he really be this sweet?

"Awesome," he said, trying to sound smooth and failing. "And like I said, it's really close to my place so we could go there to hang out before or after. I have this cool collection of Houdini memorabilia that I'm pretty proud of. It includes some rare stuff."

A little alarm went off in Alex's head at those words. This was the second time that Andy had mentioned how close he lived. Was he really just that enthused about being near the Magic Castle? Or was he trying to suggest something?

Dan had seemed like a nice, regular guy too, at least for a trick. He'd made it seem like going to his house instead of a hotel was just a matter of convenience—no big deal. And then that seemingly nice guy had tied her up and raped her.

Andy didn't seem to even know she was a prostitute. But was that true? Maybe this was his shtick, acting like the innocent geek, getting girls to let their guard down and come back to his place.

Despite all his supposed nerves, what had this guy really done? He'd approached her, charmed her, created the sense that they had something in common, asked her out and invited her back to his place. Pretty bold stuff for an outwardly tongue-tied tech nerd.

It occurred to Alex that maybe she wasn't the only "actor" at the bar. She felt her chest tightening in resentment at his manipulations and how easily she'd fallen for them.

That's what happens when you let your guard down.

"Why wait?" she said suddenly.

"What?' he asked, playing clueless.

"Why wait to show me that Houdini collection when we can go take a look at it now?"

"Are you serious?" he asked. "You really want to leave this bar and go look at my goofy magic memorabilia?"

He was really laying it on thick. But she could play that game too.

"Absolutely. No time like the present."

"Okay. Um, let me just go take care of my tab and let my friends know I'm leaving. I'll be right back. You won't disappear on me, will you?"

"I'm not going anywhere without you, cutie," she said, meaning it.

As he walked back to his buddies, Alex felt the tingle return. Tonight wasn't a lost cause after all. She'd almost fallen for his off-kilter appeal, almost allowed herself to be taken in by his goofy, faux-guileless charm.

Almost. Now her eyes were wide open to his deception. She should have anticipated this kind of thing from a guy so into magic. It was all about illusion, after all. She wasn't going to get caught unprepared again. He thought he'd drawn her into his web of lies and trickery. But she had seen through it, and just in time.

He was worse than a guy like Barry, who came on strong but at least presented himself as he really was. Andy presented himself as a wounded, fragile fawn, Bambi lost in the forest. But he was the real predator. And it was time to take this predator off the board. It was time for a Reckoning.

CHAPTER TWENTY EIGHT

Jessie didn't know where to start.

Alex's tiny room was a sea of elaborate wigs, fancy outfits that felt more like Halloween costumes than real clothes, and random items like food wrappers, a stuffed dog, makeup, and maps strewn about. Her eyes fell on the small bed, with its thin mattress on a metal frame.

The mattress must have been around forever, as it was starting to curl up a bit near the top, where a sad, half-sized pillow rested. Jessie bent down to see if there was anything hidden under the bed. She saw nothing.

But while crouched down, she noticed something she'd missed before. The mattress was actually bending upward because it appeared that there was something underneath it. She snapped on her gloves and lifted it up to discover a towel there, wrapped around something.

She picked it up and could tell immediately from the size and weight what it was: a laptop. She pulled off the towel, set it on the tiny table in the corner of the room, and opened it. It was password protected.

She sat there for a moment, imagining all the potential permutations. Normally, they'd give the computer to the tech unit and let them run a program that would eventually crack the code. But that could take hours, sometimes days. If Alex was looking for a victim tonight, and if her last two victims were any indication, they probably had about an hour before it was too late.

Jessie closed her eyes, trying to shut out everything: the shabby room with its flickering fluorescent overhead lights, the TV blaring from next door, the distant flush of the one shared toilet on the entire floor.

What password would a girl like this use? She typed in her street name—"Lexi"—and regretted it even as she hit "enter." The words "wrong password" flashed back at her.

Of course they did. This laptop belonged to Alex, not Lexi. She would never use a word associated with her current life. She wouldn't want someone who came across the laptop to even have a shot at guessing how to access it. More importantly, this wasn't the life that created her strongest memories.

It was her previous one, in Las Vegas, back when she was Alex Cutter, Mathlete and volleyball player. Back when she was part of a tandem, mom and daughter against the world, before Steve came in and corrupted their tight-knit family unit.

Jessie typed in various other options: her mom's name, "Marlene," their street name, "Oakdale," even her high school mascot, "Bulls." None of them worked.

She squeezed her eyes tighter, trying to think of something Alex would always remember, no matter how much stress she was under, a password of significance that even a cop who discovered her laptop wouldn't think of because it wasn't important to anyone but her.

She opened her eyes and scanned the room, hoping for some clue into the girl's mindset. Her attention fell on the stuffed dog and her heart almost broke at the sight of it. Alex was a murderer. But she was also a wounded, scared girl who slept in a dingy room in a crappy hotel and probably hugged her little stuffed dog tight to her at night for some semblance of comfort.

She hugs the stuffed dog here because she can't hug the real one.

Her real dog, the one she had before Steve came along, the one that Steve had killed in "self-defense" after she ran away. The dog that meant nothing to anyone else but almost certainly meant the world to her.

"What was the dog's name again?" she asked Ryan.

"What?"

"The dog Alex had in Las Vegas, the one her stepfather killed after she ran away."

"Oh," he said, struggling to recall. "I think it was Lola."

Jessie typed it in. The screen saver disappeared. She was in.

"Good job," Ryan said, impressed. "Check her web history."

"On it," Jessie said, pulling it up.

Most of her recent searches were standard fare—lots of hunting for cheap restaurants and thrift shops. There were also searches for various hotels—not just in downtown, but also Hollywood, Beverly Hills, and West LA.

Amid all the website investigations, she found a link to a chat forum titled "New Friends." She opened it and began searching Alex's chat history. It quickly became clear that this was a forum for johns to meet up with potential escorts.

Jessie couldn't help but admire the cleverness. Unlike the multiple websites, apps, and membership clubs that dominated the world of escort "dates," Alex had decided to go comparatively old school. A chat forum like "New Friends" wouldn't be easily searchable and would require prior knowledge, likely via word of mouth, to even know it existed.

Alex's comments appeared in black text under the handle "LVTrueBlue4U." Other comments were in red text. But once she opened a private, direct chat with someone, their words turned blue. The chats went back several weeks and showed that Alex had been setting up meets with clients at hotels since that time.

In each case, after agreeing to meet in person, she gave only the most basic information to the john, which included the hotel, the bar name, the time, and a general description of what she was wearing. The exchange from two nights ago read: Biltmore, Gallery Bar, 9 p.m., long blonde hair, violet dress. Last night's said: Sheraton Grand, District on the Bloc, 9 p.m. long brunette hair, yellow skirt.

And there was one from this afternoon. All it said was: Hollywood Roosevelt, Teddy's Bar, 9 p.m., long red hair, blue dress, silk scarf. Jessie checked the time. It was currently 9:41 p.m.

She looked up at Ryan, who had been reading over her shoulder. He said exactly what she was thinking.

"We've got to go."

Andy Gelman couldn't believe his luck.

He never got girls like this to take an interest in him. Despite his imminent wealth and fancy title, he was still a geek at heart. And as he'd learned repeatedly (and often embarrassingly) over the years, women who looked like the one in his house right now didn't usually go for geeks.

But for some reason Lexi seemed into him. When he'd told his buddies that she was going back home with him, Pete had high-fived him. Dell was also congratulatory, though he couldn't help but jokingly suggest that the girl was a pro.

Andy resented the insult, though he tried to hide it. Of course Dell, with his washboard abs and surfer vibe, would assume a girl this hot couldn't possibly be into a guy like him. And he had to admit the thought had occurred to him too.

But the truth was, Lexi hadn't asked for money, hadn't even hinted at such a thing. There had been no veiled references to any sexual encounter to come. She had just seemed genuinely excited to discuss old Hollywood mythology and check out his Houdini memorabilia collection.

And now, as he got drinks for them from his "bar," which consisted of a table with five bottles on it, she was eagerly flipping through a coffee table book on the famous magician.

He brought over both of their rum and Cokes and put them down on the table as he looked at the picture she was studying. It was a photo of Houdini looking dapper in a tuxedo at a party.

"You'd never know what this guy was capable of based on how he looks here," she marveled.

"Yeah, I guess that's part of what I appreciate about him. He's the ultimate example of 'don't judge a book by its cover.'"

"Words to live by," she said.

He looked over at her. Something about the seriousness and sincerity with which she'd said it made him suspect he wasn't the only one in the room who had to deal with stereotypes based on his appearance.

"You get a lot of that?" he asked before he could stop himself.

"A lot of what?"

"People judging you based on your... cover?"

She looked at him curiously for several seconds before replying.

"It's definitely a thing that happens."

"So I guess we're more alike than we seem at first glance," he said, smiling shyly.

"How's that?"

"People assume we both have to fit into a certain box based on our appearance. I guess it doesn't matter whether you look like a curly-haired version of Harry Potter or a live-action version of Jessica Rabbit."

"I guess not," she agreed, staring at him with a strange expression, one that seemed to hint at a mix of puzzlement and regret.

"Should I get out the good stuff?" he asked, trying to shake her out of her sudden melancholy.

Her face turned hard.

"I don't do drugs anymore," she said coldly.

He giggled nervously.

"I didn't mean drugs, Lexi. I'm talking about the memorabilia collection."

Her face softened slightly.

"Oh, right, of course. Please do."

He got up to access the hidden panel where he kept it. Then, realizing he'd need both hands to unlock it, he put his drink back down on the table next to Lexi's.

"This will only take a minute," he assured.

She smiled tightly. Andy understood.

She must really be nervous about seeing such valuable material.

CHAPTER TWENTY NINE

Jessie and Ryan walked into Teddy's at the Roosevelt Hotel, trying not to draw too much attention to themselves. It was 10:06 p.m.

They'd already called Hollywood Station on the drive over, asking for several plainclothes officers to go to the bar and look for anyone matching the chat forum description Alex had given of herself. If they saw her, they were not to approach her, merely observe.

They were just pulling up when they got the report that there were no obvious candidates in the bar. Jessie didn't immediately lose hope, as it was possible that Alex had decided to change her appearance between this afternoon and now. It was only when she began to circle the bar that her heart sank.

There were two redheads. But one was in her forties and the other, though the right general age, had on a black pantsuit and glasses. Her eyes were hazel and her hair was barely shoulder length.

Jessie scanned every other female in the room, focusing less on whether they matched the clothing and hair description and more on age, facial bone structure, and eye color. It took her less than a minute to dismiss every woman in the place. She reconnected with Ryan at the bar. He looked equally disappointed.

"Maybe she got cold feet," he suggested hopefully. "Or never showed up at all?"

Jessie looked at him skeptically.

"I doubt it," she said. "She's cunning. But I don't get the impression that Alex is the sort of person who can just turn herself off like that, even if she wanted to, which I don't think she does. She's committed at this point."

"Okay then," Ryan said, conceding the point. "Then let's find out if anyone saw her."

They waved down the bartender closest to them, a thirty-something woman with a ponytail and a harried expression.

"What can I get you?' she asked curtly.

"Hopefully, a positive identification," Ryan said, flashing his badge. "Have you seen a pretty redhead in here recently; blue eyes, blue dress, wearing a scarf?"

"No," she answered, apparently unfazed at being questioned by a cop. "But I only started my shift five minutes ago. Frank might know more. He's on break in the back."

They started to head in the direction she'd pointed when a guy sitting nearby leaned over.

"Did you say you were looking for a pretty redhead?" he asked. His face was flushed and his words were sloppy, as if he'd already had three too many.

"Yes," Jessie said, failing to contain her excitement. "Have you seen her?"

His friend, equally sauced, piped up.

"Yeah, she was frickin' hot," he said, before realizing he was being indiscreet. "I mean, she was very attractive, ma'am, like you."

"Describe her," Ryan said, pretending to ignore the last comment.

"Really blue eyes, slammin' body," the second guy said, quickly forgetting his earlier attempt at gentlemanliness. "We were both blown away when she started flirting with Andy."

"Who's Andy?" Jessie asked.

"He's our buddy," the first guy said. "She was giving him a look so he went over and they started talking, really seemed to hit it off."

"I told you, man," the second guy, who looked to Jessie like a surfer out of his element in this high-brow cocktail bar, said. "I think that chick makes a living out of hitting it off with any guy."

"What do you mean?" Jessie asked.

"Dell was sure she was a pro," the first guy said. "But I don't know. She seemed to really like Andy. And he said she never mentioned money. She just wanted to see his Houdini stuff."

"What?" Ryan asked.

"Yeah, man," the one apparently named Dell said. "Andy's got this collection of crap on this old magician-daredevil guy named Harry Houdini. He says it's super valuable but it doesn't look like much to me. Anyway, he said she was into seeing it. So they went back to his place. We're hoping he gets to work a little magic of his own."

"Where is Andy's place?" Jessie demanded.

"Like three blocks from here," Dell said.

"We need the address, now!"

Alex almost left the apartment.

The whole evening was a roller-coaster of emotions. One minute, she was ready to do what had to be done. The next she was full of doubt, asking if this guy was really like the others.

Even back at his place, he hadn't made a move. She could tell that he was into her. He had that nervous energy all guys got when they were alone with her. But other than that, he hadn't given any outward indication that he was like the others.

And yet, he'd charmed her into the back room of his apartment, the one with the heavy door and no windows. Sure, he said that was to protect his most prized passion—the Houdini collection. But it also made it easy to trap an unsuspecting girl.

Plus, he'd offered her a drink as soon as they walked in, usually a sign that he wanted to lower her inhibitions. Or he could just be polite. He'd sat down next to her on the loveseat, the only option in the room. But he'd asked permission first and even then, he'd left her some personal space. He was either the sweetest guy she'd met in Los Angeles or the sneakiest.

It was moot anyway. When he'd gotten up to unlock his Houdini safe, she'd poured the sedative into his drink. He seemed okay now as he guided her through the (surprisingly interesting) artifacts from some of Houdini's coolest stunts. But any second now, he'd start slurring his words. His movements would get clumsy. He'd grow weak. And then, the Reckoning could begin.

Andy tried to stay cool.

This girl was almost too good to be true. Painfully beautiful, with eyes that pierced right through him and a figure he was hesitant to look at directly, she was also genuinely interested in the kind of obscure stuff he found fascinating. She'd even put on some latex gloves she happened to have with her so as not to get her skin oils on the old material. She seemed to have appeared out of a dream.

Yet she was real. And unless he was imagining it, as he described Houdini's New York midair, upside-down subway crane, straitjacket escape, she seemed to be inching closer to him on the loveseat so that there was no longer any unoccupied space between them.

And then, as if to prove it wasn't his imagination, she put her hand on his leg. He felt a ripple of electricity course through him and heard himself stop talking. He could feel her eyes on him and almost, scared, looked over at her.

"Maybe we should take a little break," she purred.

"Okay," he replied hoarsely, his voice cracking a little.

Before he knew what was happening, she leaned into him and her warm lips were pressed against his. He lost his balance slightly and toppled back on the loveseat. She didn't seem to mind, climbing on top of him and giggling slightly as she nibbled at his neck.

She had gone from coy to ravenous in moments. And while he wasn't upset about it, he was a little confused. Had he said or done something to turn a switch on in her? And if so, what was it and how could he replicate it?

Stop asking questions. Just go with it.

He was so annoyed with himself that he actually shook his head slightly in frustration. To his surprise, it didn't move immediately on command. His skull felt slightly heavier than usual, like someone had strapped a ten-pound helmet to it.

"You okay?" Lexi asked, briefly stopping what she was doing to his earlobe.

"Yeah, I'm good," he said, not wanting to mess up the moment by telling her that he actually felt a bit woozy.

"You *are* good," she murmured as she kissed the top of his chest.

When her lips bumped up against his shirt collar, she sat up and simply ripped the thing open. Buttons popped, flying everywhere. Her arm bumped into his tumbler, knocking it off the coffee table. He heard it break into several pieces on the floor but Lexi seemed oblivious. She smiled at him greedily before diving back toward him, licking her way down.

Andy looked up at the ceiling, stunned at the sudden turn of events. This might be the best day ever: successful IPO followed by meeting a sexy, geeky girl who wanted to ravage him. He was so amped that he feared it might be affecting his vision, which was slightly blurry. The overhead light seemed to be shifting in and out of focus.

Then, to his horror, he found that he was getting sleepy. This could not be happening now. He decided he needed to take a more active role in events, if for no other reason than to shake off this unexpected drowsiness.

He tried to slide his arms up so that he could push off and sit up slightly. He was surprised to discover that they wouldn't move. He glanced down at his right hand and ordered it to turn palm down so that he could push up. It didn't respond. In fact, now that he thought about it, his whole body felt weighted down and unresponsive. He couldn't feel Lexi's tongue on his skin anymore.

"Something's wrong," he said, noticing that his own tongue seemed to be fighting him.

Lexi looked up.

"What is it?' she asked, her voice like warm honey.

"I feels funny," he said with great effort. "Everything heavy."

She sat up, still straddling him, with a concerned look on her face. Grabbing his right arm, she lifted it into the air.

"Keep this up," she instructed and let go.

His arm flopped back onto the couch.

"You're right," she said. "Are you allergic to something?"

"Peanoots . . ."

"I don't think there were any peanuts in that drink," she said, smiling sympathetically. "Maybe someone slipped you something."

The way she said it, as if she'd been waiting to speak those words, sent a chill down Andy's spine. He was surprised he could even feel that.

"Whaa mean?" he managed to garble out.

Lexi looked down at him silently. He couldn't understand her expression. She was smiling but there were tears in her eyes, which were exuding a combination of anticipation and sadness. Finally she spoke.

"I'm so sorry, Andy," she said softly. "I'm sorry it had to be you."

"Whaaa...?"

His whole body was clammy now and, though he couldn't feel it, he was sure he was sweating. He was consumed by a mix of confusion, fear, and nausea.

"I did this to you," she said as she climbed off him and took off his shoes and socks. She unbuttoned his pants and pulled them down to reveal his Mickey Mouse boxers. Seeing them made her giggle slightly before she stifled a sob. "Oh, you are making this so difficult."

She slid his arms out of his shirt and placed them gently back on the love-seat. Then she looked down at floor. He followed her gaze to the pieces of glass from the broken tumbler. She seemed to sense he was watching her and looked back at over at him.

"Don't worry," she told him soothingly. "Stabbing is not my style. I'm more hands on."

Despite the outside of his body being completely numb, Andy felt his insides clench up in terror.

CHAPTER THIRTY

A lex wasn't enjoying this.

There was none of the thrill from the previous Reckonings. Usually she lingered on each moment leading up to the kill, luxuriating in teasing her victim as he lay helpless, feeding off the dread rising from his body like steam on a winter's day.

But right now, she was consumed by conflicting emotions. Part of her wanted to complete the task, to get the high that could only come from snuffing out the life of a perpetrator. And yet, despite what she told herself, a nagging thought kept darting into her brain.

What if he's not like them?

This man, more a boy still really, had never said or done anything to suggest he deserved this fate. He seemed to be innocent of the crimes she wanted to punish him for. And yet...

He'd been in the bar. He'd hit on her. He'd invited her back to his place. He clearly had an agenda and it wasn't to look at memorabilia all night. And when she'd jumped him he hadn't protested or suggested they wait until they knew each other better. He was a willing participant. In fact, based on his involuntary reaction when she'd climbed on top of him, he was an enthusiastic one. Andy was no angel.

It didn't matter anyway. He'd already taken the dose. Unless he got the antidote medication, called flumazenil, which she didn't have, he'd be dead in a few minutes anyway. She'd already started this process. It was time to finish it. Honor demanded it.

She wiped the tears away from her cheeks and smiled down at Andy, who was frozen except for his uncomprehending eyes and his wordless, rasping lips. This time when she smiled, it finally felt right—ruthless and triumphant.

"It has to be done, Andy," she said as she carefully adjusted her gloves. "I wish I could tell you it won't hurt. But even with the drugs, it will. That's kind of the point, actually—for you to hurt. It's only fair."

He blinked desperately at her and she knew what it meant. He was giving her one last plea to stop. She admired the effort.

But the time for stopping had passed. Dan hadn't stopped when she begged him to. Her stepfather hadn't stopped when she pleaded with him. He hadn't stopped when she agreed to be quiet so as not to "upset her mother" in the next bedroom. No one ever stopped with her. So why should she?

She'd stop when she was done.

Jessie didn't want to wait.

On the two-minute drive over, after calling for reinforcements, Ryan had suggested they hold off on breaking through the door of Andy Gelman's apartment until they had the tactical entry battering ram. She understood the argument. They wanted to get in fast and clean so that Alex couldn't use any delay in entry to harm Andy Gelman.

But she was worried they might already be too late. Andy's friends said they left the bar over forty minutes ago. That was more than enough time to return to his apartment, drug him, and strangle him. Any delay could be the difference between life and death.

They agreed to decide on how to proceed when they saw how heavy the front door of his apartment was. After they pulled up, hopped out of the car, and sprinted up to the building, they saw that the complex was protected by a security gate.

Jessie, whose feet still throbbed from hours of searching downtown motels, was debating whether they should just shoot the lock when Ryan grabbed hold of the bars and leapt up, scaling the eight-foot wall as if it was nothing. He dropped down the other side and pushed open the door for Jessie, who stared at him in amazement.

"Cross training," he said, grinning, then turned and hurried into the complex.

The building had four stories and Andy's was on the second, in unit 207. As they rushed down the hall, Ryan turned back and whispered to Jessie.

"The doors aren't that impressive. I think I can bust it in with one kick."

She nodded back, too out of breath to reply. She still wasn't totally back in shape from her recent injuries. When they got to unit 207, they paused for a moment, each trying to get their wind back, if only briefly.

After what amounted to three seconds, Ryan gave her the "you ready?" look and she nodded. They both pulled out their weapons.

"Open up, police," Ryan shouted quickly even as he kicked the door.

It flew open and they both rushed in. Jessie went left as Ryan took the right side of the apartment. There was a small sitting room with an open door leading to the empty kitchen. She stepped back into the center hall where she met Ryan again as he exited an apparently unoccupied bedroom after having cleared the living room. They passed the dining nook and Jessie checked the bathroom while Ryan searched the master bedroom. They both came out shaking their heads.

As they heard the sound of other officers running down the hall, they both looked at the last unopened door in the apartment. It was heavy-looking and at first, Jessie thought they would need the battering ram. But then she noticed that it was actually slightly ajar, which she found odd. If Alex was in there, wouldn't she have locked it to give herself time to escape?

Ryan indicated for her to push it open so he could dive in first. She nodded and gave the door a shove. As it swung open, he rolled in somersault-style and popped up impressively. Jessie followed, though without the acrobatics.

It took a moment to fully comprehend the scene in front of her. Lying on his back on a loveseat at the other end of the room was a young man she assumed was Andy Gelman. He was naked except for a pair of boxers. His eyes were flittering open and shut as if he was on the verge of falling asleep.

Crouched on top of him, in a blue dress, was Alex Cutter. She was holding what looked like a shard of glass to Andy's carotid artery, her eyes darting back and forth between the two people pointing guns at her. It was also clear why she hadn't locked herself in. There were no windows in the room. There was no escape.

Even in this moment, Jessie was upended by how stunning the young woman was. She looked like something out of the *Sports Illustrated* swimsuit issue, curves everywhere. Despite the nature of the situation, the girl somehow looked above it all, with her defined cheekbones, regal chin, and delicate, refined nose. None of the horrors she'd experienced seemed to have done anything to muddy her pristine features.

Jessie did note the nickel-sized scar on the girl's left shoulder, about the size of a cigar butt or a car cigarette lighter. The deep indentation suggested it hadn't gotten there by accident.

And then there were the eyes—relentlessly clear and blue, sparkling like sapphires in the room's dull light. They seemed to be lit from within and Jessie felt like she was undergoing an X-ray via the girl's gaze.

Those eyes were shockingly tranquil, considering the situation. Alex didn't look panicked by their arrival, or even all that surprised to see them. Jessie heard officers pouring into the apartment and glanced over at Ryan.

"You've got to hold the reinforcements back," she said quietly to him. "I need a little quiet time in here."

He nodded and took a step back so that he could see down the hallway and keep an eye on Alex.

"Stay back," he yelled at the approaching officers. "The suspect is holding a weapon to the victim's throat. Remain outside the room."

After a moment of silence, Alex spoke.

"Of course you'd think *he* was the victim," she muttered sharply.

Jessie looked at the girl and decided she needed to do something to change the dynamic. Knowing Ryan still had his gun trained on the young woman, she holstered hers and took a tiny step forward. She had to handle this delicately.

"We think he's one of the victims," she said softly. "But we know he isn't the only one."

"Sure," Alex replied derisively. "You found the others. But I wouldn't call them victims either."

"No," Jessie said, fully aware that her next words were crucial. "I was talking about you, Alex."

The girl's face remained unchanged but Jessie saw flash of surprise in her eyes.

"My name is Lexi," she insisted.

"That may be your name now. But that's not who you truly are. You're Alexis Cutter, former volleyball player and Mathlete, daughter to Marlene and loving caretaker of Lola. That's who you really are."

"That person doesn't exist anymore," she nearly spat back, her hand pressing the glass closer to Andy's neck.

As she said it, she pushed her mane of red hair out of her eyes. That gave Jessie an idea but she waited a moment before pursuing it. When she was sure the girl wasn't going to push the glass any farther, she continued.

"I think she does," Jessie insisted. "Steve Kupisch tried to erase her. So did Daniel Beane. But I think she's still in there. I think that's why you sleep with that little stuffed dog at night. I think that's why you haven't killed Andy yet—because Alex is still in there somewhere."

"You're wrong," the girl said firmly, though with less vitriol than before.

"I don't think I am. That's why, if you took off that wig, I suspect we'd find that your real color is the same one you had back in high school, the same blonde hair you had in the volleyball games and math competitions. Am I right, Alex?"

The girl stared at her for several seconds. Then, without a word, she pulled off the red wig to reveal a shock of short, spiky blonde hair. She dropped the wig on the ground with a defiant glare. Jessie chose to interpret the action as a sign of hope.

"Listen, Alex," she said gently. "I've been through some pretty terrible stuff in my life. But I can't pretend to understand the horrors you've suffered. The people you were supposed to depend on betrayed and violated you. You were trapped by a system that assumed the worst about you. You had to do things to survive that I can barely comprehend."

"You have no idea," Alex said through gritted teeth.

"No, I don't," Jessie admitted. "But I know you're a victim of a world that used and abused you. I get it. I understand that to get up every day, you had to find some way to move forward, to function in the hell that was your daily life. I get all that. And you know what, Alex? I think a jury will too."

"What are you talking about?"

Jessie stopped inching forward, aware that she'd reached a sensitive, if inevitable moment. But Andy's eyes were no longer fluttering. They hadn't moved in several seconds. Jessie feared that unless they got him help soon, he wouldn't make it.

"I think that when you go on trial and a jury hears about what you've been through the last three years, they will understand why you made some of the choices you made. That doesn't mean it can all be washed away. But they might take pity on you..."

"I don't want anyone's pity," Alex growled.

"Maybe not out here," Jessie replied. "But in that courtroom, you will. You'll want them to give you a reduced sentence or put you in a facility where you can get therapy. They might even cut you loose. Have you ever heard of jury nullification?"

Alex shook her head.

"It means that the jury refuses to convict someone, even if they think they're guilty of the crime. Like a father who kills the man who murdered his child. I'm not saying they'd do that with you. But it's not impossible, unless you make it impossible."

Despite her best efforts to hide it, Alex was clearly curious.

"What does that mean?" she asked.

"It means that no jury is going to have much sympathy for you if you kill Andy. He didn't abuse you. He didn't assault you. He didn't even solicit you for prostitution. According to his friends at the bar, he didn't even know you're an escort. He's just a regular guy who's way too into Harry Houdini. He doesn't deserve this."

"He deserves a Reckoning," Alex whispered, her hand now digging the glass harder into Andy's neck.

Jessie saw a trickle of blood snake down his neck and forced herself to look back at the penetrating eyes of the girl who'd done that.

"No, Alex, he doesn't. Killing him won't make up for what happened to you. It doesn't give you more power to harm an innocent person. You know who it gives power to? Your stepfather. If you kill this boy, then Steve wins. He will have corrupted you and made you like him. I know you think you're meting out justice. But vengeance and justice are not the same thing."

"I don't see the difference anymore," Alex sobbed.

"I don't believe that," Jessie said adamantly. "You want justice. Your stepfather is sitting in prison right now, awaiting trial for assaulting a girl like you. You know that. Surrender now. Agree to testify against him, to tell the world what he did to you. He's planning to argue that he's not capable of hurting some young girl. But we both know that's not true. You can tell the truth, Alex, You can speak for her. But if you do this tonight, no one will listen."

Alex's beautiful eyes were brimming with tears. She looked down at Andy, now deathly pale, and back up at Jessie. Then, without a word, she tossed the glass away.

CHAPTER THIRTY ONE

A ndy barely made it.

The EMTs swarmed in as soon as Alex was in custody and gave him a dose of flumazenil. Within a minute he was conscious. But they stayed put for several minutes after that, watching him closely for signs of seizures, a danger-ous potential side effect of the antidote medication. When they were sure he was in the clear on that score, they wheeled him out of the apartment. Jessie heard him clumsily trying to speak, which she considered a good sign.

She waited until Alex had been handcuffed and read her rights, then walked her outside. The girl seemed to be in a state of shock, alternately crying and going silent, her blue eyes blank. Jessie whispered to her that they would get her help, that they would find her a therapist, and that she would get a chance to testify against her stepfather.

And when she was sure they were out of earshot of Ryan, whom she doubted would approve, Jessie whispered one more thing. She told Alex not to speak to anyone about anything until she'd gotten an attorney.

The girl looked over at her, surprised. For the first time, Jessie could tell she'd truly won the girl's trust. Alex nodded her understanding as the officers escorting her eased her into the back of a squad car. And then, in a cascade of sirens and lights, they sped away, leaving Jessie alone beside Ryan.

"You told her not to talk, didn't you?" he asked.

"I just reminded her of her rights," Jessie said, not looking at him. "My job was to catch her, not convict her."

"You know it's not as simple as that, right?" he replied, sounding less angry than frustrated.

"We caught her in the act, Ryan. Her most recent victim will be able to testify against her. She's not going free. But this girl can be rehabilitated. She needs help, not to be thrown into a hole."

"Are you sure she's not going free? What about that whole jury nullification thing you mentioned to her?"

"We both know that's not going to happen," she said.

"Do we?" Ryan challenged. "I've seen it happen before. But this isn't some grieving parent avenging their murdered child. She's a serial killer, Jessie."

"That's why we need to do our part to ensure she ends up in a secure facility that can help her."

"You mean like NRD?" he asked. "That place was supposed to be secure and Bolton Crutchfield got out, along with a bunch of other killers. And we both know the consequences of that."

"You're not really comparing Alex Cutter to Bolton Crutchfield, are you?" she asked angrily.

But Ryan didn't back down.

"How do we know what Bolton was like at eighteen? He was abused, right? Maybe he started out like her, just fighting to survive. But once he got a taste for killing, there was no going back. Can you honestly say she's not the same?"

Jessie looked at him. It was clear that this wasn't a philosophical debate for him. He'd seen too many murderers skate on technicalities or clever lawyering, only to kill again, to have faith in the power of rehabilitation.

The truth was she wasn't much more confident. But she needed to believe that people could rise above their circumstances. It wasn't just theory to her either. Right now, her half-sister was in the clutches of a serial killer trying to mold her in his image. If Jessie was able to find and rescue her, Hannah would likely need an entire team to deprogram her and make her a functional member of society. Was that a lost cause? She had to believe it wasn't.

"This is raw right now," she finally said. "Let's leave it for tonight. There will be lots of time to argue about this in the weeks ahead. I don't have the energy to do it now. Truce?"

He looked at her and she watched his face soften, despite his best efforts to prevent it.

"Truce," he said. "Let's go back to the station and finish the paperwork. Then we can sleep in a bit tomorrow."

"Deal," she said getting in the passenger seat and strapping in.

As Ryan drove, Jessie checked her messages, hoping for a message from Garland Moses. But there was nothing from him. In fact, she found nothing at all in the way of messages other than a LinkedIn invitation.

More as a way to keep her anxiety at bay than out of genuine curiosity, she clicked on it. When the message opened, she nearly dropped her phone.

"What is it?" Ryan asked when he heard her gasp.

"It's a LinkedIn invite from Robert Rylance," she said, trying to calm her quickly palpitating heart.

"Isn't that the guy from Redlands that Moses suggested you look into as a possible victim?"

"Yes," she confirmed, her mind racing.

"But I thought that ended up being a dead end."

"I did too," she admitted. "But I think there might be something to it."

"You've lost me," he said.

Jessie looked over at him and realized the time had arrived to come clean or cut him out completely.

"Ryan," she said, carefully calibrating each word, "I can clear things up. But I'm not sure you want me to."

"That sounds ominous."

"You've got a choice to make," she said, ignoring his comment. "We can go to the station where I'll drop you off to do the case paperwork and, no questions asked, I'll go on my way to deal with a situation that's come up. Or we can skip the station entirely and you can join me on my errand while I fill you in on what I think is going on. But that could have career consequences you might not want. It's a decision only you can make."

"What is this?" he asked, trying to keep some levity in his voice. "It sounds like you're asking if I want to take the red pill or the blue pill."

"I kind of am," she said, without a trace of humor.

He sat quietly for several seconds, the only sound the car tires on the darkened street. Then, without taking his eyes off the road, he replied.

"Give me the red pill."

CHAPTER THIRTY TWO

The freeway was nearly empty.

As they traveled down the I-10 eastward to Redlands, Ryan didn't even need to turn on the siren. There were so few cars that the flashing lights he used might not even have been necessary. At the rate they were going, Jessie estimated they'd be to their destination in less than a half hour.

Before explaining everything else, Jessie read Ryan the LinkedIn message. It was short:

Hope to meet soon. We could discuss the Bare Essence, like Catcher in the Rye.

"Robert Rylance sent that to you?" Ryan asked, confused.

"I don't think so," she answered, still working out the theory in her own head, even as she shared it with him. "My suspicion is that the message is actually from Hannah."

"But how is Hannah connected to a guy Moses thinks Alex Cutter tried to take out?"

"Okay," Jessie began hesitantly. "Here's the part where you might get pissed. I've been holding out on you. I couldn't pursue the investigation into Hannah's abduction. Captain Decker made that very clear. So I went to Garland Moses and asked if he could poke around. He's not officially precluded from reviewing the case. And he's friendly with several FBI agents working it. He agreed to look into it, though he warned me he'd have to be delicate about it."

"And he found something?" Ryan asked, swerving across three lanes to avoid several eighteen-wheelers in a small convoy.

With each passing second, Jessie was increasingly confident that he had.

"I didn't think so at first," she said, trying to keep her voice even. "He gave me a lead. But he suggested it was related to the hotel murders. I think he said that in part to cover his own ass, but mostly so I could investigate without attracting attention, without even knowing I was looking into Hannah's case."

"So Rylance isn't related to Alex at all?"

"I don't think so," Jessie said. "I think something about the details surrounding Rylance's disappearance made Moses suspect a link to Crutchfield. I'm not sure what. But whatever it was, I think he used the hotel murders as an excuse to get me to look into what happened to him. Unfortunately, I never made the connection."

"So what makes you think they're related now?"

What does make me think that?

Of course she knew the answer. After all, that answer was the hopeful hypothesis making her stomach currently twist in a knot of excitement and anxiety. She was almost reluctant to say it out loud for fear that the words would lose credibility when exposed to the air. Nonetheless, she pressed on.

"When I was coming back from Redlands, I noticed lots of billboards for strip clubs," she told him. "One of them was called Bare Essence. In the LinkedIn invitation, the reference to 'Bare Essence' is capitalized, which seems intentional. It struck me as too much of a coincidence to get that exact phrase from a guy who lives so close to a club with that name."

"Okay," Ryan said, nodding in understanding. "That makes sense. But I still don't get why you think this is connected to Hannah. Couldn't it just be Rylance sending you a coded message asking for help?"

Jessie took a deep breath. This was the leap of faith moment. She hoped he'd take it with her.

"I think it is a coded message, but not from Rylance. I've never met him. I had no idea who he was until yesterday and I doubt he knows of me. But Hannah does. And when I visited her at her foster home, she was lying in a hammock, reading. The book was *Catcher in the Rye*."

Jessie saw Ryan's whole body stiffen. He said nothing so she continued.

"I think Crutchfield abducted Rylance and was keeping him at the same location as her. I think she somehow got a hold of his phone and sent me this message in the only way she knew how. She didn't have my phone number or e-mail or anything else. So she found the LinkedIn app on Rylance's phone and searched for me. I have a profile on there. Decker made me create one, though I haven't looked at it in weeks. I think she kept the message vague in case Crutchfield found it."

"Why didn't she just call nine-one-one?" Ryan asked.

"Who knows? Maybe Crutchfield was nearby and she didn't want to risk having him hear voices. Maybe she was worried they wouldn't believe her. Maybe she couldn't get a good cell connection. Regardless, she's the only person who would have known to reference that book *and* the strip club. It must be close enough to where he's holding her that she can see it."

"So just to be clear," Ryan said, "based only on this message, you think that Hannah's being held somewhere in the immediate vicinity of a Redlands strip club?"

"I'm sure of it."

Bare Essence was located in an industrial section of Redlands, about a mile off the freeway. They passed two other strip clubs on the way there, along with a foundry, three other factories, and multiple abandoned warehouses.

The sign for the club itself was visible from a quarter mile away. It flashed the name "Bare Essence" in alternating pink and blue neon script that lit up the surrounding block like something out of a rural version of *Blade Runner*.

They pulled up into the massive lot, easily the size of a city block, which was surprisingly full for a Wednesday. An attendant tried to charge them $7 until Ryan flashed his badge. Once in the lot, they rolled over dirt and gravel to the far end, trying to avoid countless potholes along the way.

Jessie looked at the time. It was already 1:33 a.m. The club would be closing in twenty-seven minutes. They needed to find where Hannah was soon, before the neon sign was shut off. Once that happened they'd have no way to gauge which locations had a clear visual of it until sunrise.

"I'm thinking we check houses," Ryan suggested. "The only other options are that warehouse down the way and the liquor store on the corner. I doubt he stashed her in either of those."

"I get the liquor store but why not the warehouse?"

"When we drove by, I noticed that several doors were open or missing entirely and some windows were broken. That's a hard place to secure under the best of circumstances, and especially if you're trying to hide two people there."

"Makes sense," Jessie agreed. "So, the neighborhood then?"

They both looked over at the residential area a few hundred yards to the east. Calling it a neighborhood was generous. It was basically a dozen homes, most no larger than trailers. Even from this distance Jessie could see it was run down. Several houses had dilapidated sheds in the open yards and one in the distance even seemed to have the remnants of a barn.

"The neighborhood," Ryan said. "Just let me call it in first."

Jessie put her hand on his before he spoke into the radio.

"Are we sure that's a good idea?" she asked. "I wouldn't put it past Crutchfield to be checking the scanner. And even if he isn't, I worry they'll come in too loud and inadvertently warn him."

"Okay," Ryan conceded. "Then I'll call the police chief personally and insist they come in quiet. I'll warn him to give instructions through alternate methods and be vague about the location on the radio. Fair?"

"Fair," Jessie said, though she had her doubts about Chief Stoller's willingness to adhere to instructions from a fancy LAPD detective. But at this point, they couldn't be choosy about their backup.

To her surprise, Stoller sounded amenable to Ryan's request. Maybe the late hour had convinced him to take the situation seriously. After the call, Ryan suggested they start at the south end and work their way north. Jessie had another idea.

"I was thinking we should start at opposite ends and work our way to the center," she countered.

Ryan looked appalled at the suggestion.

"We don't know the area. I don't want him getting the jump on one of us alone."

"He doesn't know we're coming," Jessie reminded him. "There's no reason he'd be in a position to do that. Besides, we have limited time before they turn off that sign. If we split up, we can cover the territory twice as fast. It's only about six houses each."

Ryan looked unenthused but reluctantly agreed.

"We check in after we clear every house, okay?" he insisted.

"Sounds good. Remember, the house needs to have a clear sight line to the strip club or at least to the sign. We should look for windows facing that direction."

"Agreed," Ryan said. "Which end do you want to start at?"

"Doesn't matter. I guess I can start at the north end, closest to the street. But let's get started. I'm still worried those cops will show up with sirens blaring and tip Crutchfield off."

Ryan nodded, held up his phone to remind her to stay in constant contact, pulled out his gun, and headed south. Jessie removed hers as well, turned, and walked toward the northernmost house, which looked more like a small garage with a chimney. She dismissed it as the likely home immediately as it had no doors or windows facing the club's sign.

She texted that info to Ryan and moved to the next home. It looked away from the club but did have one window facing it. The window was half-open and she was able to push the curtain aside and peek in. She was looking into an empty kitchen, hardly a likely place to keep people hidden. She texted that to Ryan, who responded that he'd come up empty with his first house.

She followed the same procedure with the next two houses. One had no club-facing doors or windows. She passed that along to Ryan, who indicated that his second house was a bust.

Her next house did have windows. But they were uncovered and she could see in, where an elderly man had fallen asleep in front of the television, which was blaring some medical drama rerun. She texted that to Ryan and moved to the fifth house.

She was now close enough that she could see his half of the neighborhood.

"I'm close," she texted. "Where are you?"

She waited several seconds but there was no response.

"Ryan?" she texted again as she looked into the candy-colored night for any sign of him.

Finally, after another thirty seconds, a one-word text appeared: "colder."

What the hell does that mean?

"Where are you?' she responded as quick as her fingers would move.

After another half minute a new text came through. It read: "your beau is currently indisposed."

Jessie stifled a gasp.

CHAPTER THIRTY THREE

Jessie suddenly felt her body explode with adrenaline. She knew that phrasing. The text wasn't from Ryan. It was from Crutchfield.

Instinctively, she raised her gun and peered in every direction, looking for any sign of either man. But there was nothing.

She ordered herself to slow her breathing and think clearly.

He has Ryan. You can't do anything about that now. He doesn't have you. Keep it that way. Stay alert. Find him.

She forced her legs to move in the direction of Ryan's set of houses, looking for any clues as to where he might have gone. When she got to the third house, she found one. Along the side of the house were two sets of fresh track marks.

One was shoeprints, seemingly walking backward. The other looked to be drag marks, as if the first person was pulling the second. That was consistent with the theory that Crutchfield had killed or knocked out Ryan and dragged him somewhere.

Knocked out. Not dead. Crutchfield said "currently" indisposed, not permanently.

She made the decision to believe this as she followed the tracks, which led eastward toward the lonely, dilapidated, barn-like building at the far end of the neighborhood. It was only when she got closer that she realized there was another structure behind it.

They'd missed it before because it was blocked by the barn. But beyond it was another house. It looked much like the others, if perhaps a little larger. It had multiple windows facing the strip club sign. And as she got closer, Jessie noticed one other thing. It appeared to have a basement.

Near the base of the house was one small window that served no purpose in its location unless it offered some light and air to a room below the ground.

Basements were rare in Southern California. But it made sense for Crutchfield to have one.

They were naturally soundproof and since they were so uncommon, the room could be concealed and most folks wouldn't even realize it existed. It was the perfect place to hide something or someone.

As Jessie approached, she saw the track marks go straight to the front door of the house, where they stopped. Crutchfield had taken Ryan inside. Jessie took some comfort in the fact that she hadn't seen any blood on the walk here. But other than that, the situation was bleak.

She'd lost both the element of surprise and her partner. Crutchfield was waiting inside a house that he'd likely booby-trapped, where Hannah was a hostage. He was very likely watching her now as she crept forward.

That's when she had an epiphany. There was no point in hiding or sneaking around. Every advantage she thought she had was now gone. If she, Hannah, and Ryan were going to survive this, she needed to change the rules of the game.

So she holstered her gun, stood up straight, and called out in the direction of the house.

"This is rude, Bolton," she said, using his first name. "Don't you think you should invite me in?"

It only took a second to get a reply.

"I'm otherwise engaged, Miss Jessie. But the door is unlocked. Please see yourself in. And I think everyone in here would appreciate it if you left your weapons outside."

Jessie removed her gun again and placed it on the ground beside her.

"Do I really have to say it, Miss Jessie? All your weapons, and your phone."

She smiled slightly as she lifted the bottom of her pant leg and removed a pistol from her ankle holster. She put it down next to her other gun, then placed the phone beside it.

"Thank you," he said. "Now please come on inside. I'll direct you from there."

"How do I know you haven't booby-trapped the place?' she yelled.

"I most certainly have," he called back. "But if it sets your mind at ease, please know that I've temporarily disabled them for our reunion. I don't want you accidentally blowing your own head off."

With no choice but to believe him, Jessie walked forward, took the single step leading up to the house, and grabbed the doorknob. She was fully aware that Crutchfield could shoot her the second she stepped through the door.

But she reminded herself that he could have already done that from a window. He could have done it after he took out Ryan. He could have done it on multiple other occasions in recent months. And yet he never had.

She knew he liked her. In fact, there were several instances in which he'd actually saved her by warning her about threats from others, including her own father, who had been his mentor in murder. That decision had put him in Xander's crosshairs and would have likely led to a confrontation between the two men if Jessie hadn't gotten to her father first.

But this felt different. Crutchfield had kidnapped her half-sister. He'd taken her partner. He was coming after her in ways he'd never done before. Despite their past détente, it would be foolish to assume that his intentions now were anything other than malevolent. With that in mind, she opened the door and stepped inside.

The living room was mostly dark, save for one dim lamp in the corner. It was a dramatic change from the artificial sun afforded by the strip club sign. Jessie stood still, waiting for her eyes to adjust. Even before they did, she heard her next instruction.

"Head straight ahead to the kitchen and look to the left," Crutchfield's staticky voice said.

She did as he ordered, walking through an open doorway into the kitchen. On the breakfast table was a walkie-talkie. To her left was a closed door.

"Open the door."

As she did, she wasn't surprised to find a set of stairs leading down into what had to be the basement. The voice crackled through the walkie-talkie.

"Jessie Hunt," Crutchfield said in his best game show voice, "come on down!"

Reluctantly, she did, carefully navigating the rickety wooden stairs, lit only by a single bulb dangling from the ceiling. When she reached the bottom of the stairs, she looked around, trying to discern the forms hidden in the shadows.

After a moment, she was able to identify a few. She saw two unmoving males lying on the ground. One appeared to be Robert Rylance. He was strapped to a chair, surrounded by what looked to be a mostly dried up pool of blood.

The other figure was Ryan, who lay crumpled on the ground, his wrists and ankles bound. She told herself that Crutchfield wouldn't have felt the need to tie him up if he was already dead. That and the continued lack of blood gave her some dim hope that her partner, friend, and maybe more might survive this after all. She looked up. Though it was too dark to tell for sure, she could sense there were others in the room too.

As if on cue, two people moved forward into the light. To Jessie's relief, she saw that one of them was Hannah. The brief moment of respite was almost immediately undercut when she saw Hannah's situation. The girl was standing in front of Crutchfield, who had one arm wrapped around her chest. His other hand was holding a long hunting knife to her throat, just as he had been in Jessie's nightmare.

"Welcome to my humble abode," he said, smiling, revealing his uneven, yellow teeth.

He looked just as she remembered. He still had the pudgy face that made him look significantly younger than his thirty-six years. His brown hair was still neatly parted to the side. And his brown eyes still stared at her like a wolf studying its prey.

Hannah, for her part, looked less comfortable. Her blondish hair was matted and her green eyes were red, with dark circles below them. She looked like she might collapse if Crutchfield released his grip on her.

All the way into the house and down the stairs, Jessie had been internally debating how to proceed. Crutchfield fancied himself a gentleman and liked it when he was able to engage in the formalities he felt he was entitled to. He also liked to play games, tease, and cajole. This whole setup was an elaborate unnecessary game, after all.

Was she better off feeding into that, stalling until the cops got here? It was an option but she feared it would only delay the inevitable. When the police eventually came storming down those stairs, he would slit Hannah's throat, game or not.

It seemed like the wiser move might be to play into his sense of fair play, to ask him to replace Hannah with herself. She could remind him that his beef was with her, not a teenager. If she could trade herself for her half-sister, then at least she thought she had a shot against the guy.

At five-eight and 150 pounds, he was actually shorter, if heavier than her. And she had continued to train in the self-defense techniques she'd learned at the FBI Academy. If things got physical, at least she'd have a fighting chance. She couldn't say the same for Hannah.

"It *is* a humble abode," Jessie finally agreed. "I thought when you invited me to your home, it would be in the southern plantation style."

"We make do with what's available to us," he said, mock-apologetically.

Jessie proceeded cautiously. She wanted to keep him on edge but not push too hard.

"Well, I appreciate that these are unusual circumstances," she said. "But I hate to think what assumptions Hannah must be making about your neighborliness, considering the house and, you know, the knife pressed to her neck. Maybe you could send her on her way and you and I could discuss things by ourselves. I think that might help improve her view of your hospitality."

Crutchfield half-giggled at the suggestion.

"Oh, I think Miss Hannah is perfectly happy here with us," he said giddily.

"Is that true, Hannah?" Jessie asked.

Hannah glanced back at Crutchfield, checking to see if she was permitted to speak.

"It's okay, dear," he assured her. "Tell her how you're doing."

Hannah started to talk, but then broke off into a coughing jag. Crutchfield moved the knife ever so slightly away so as not to inadvertently nick her. After regrouping, Hannah tried again.

"You know," she began, her voice dry and raspy, "I've obviously been better. But compared to that guy, I'm doing okay." Her glance downward indicated that she was referencing Rylance.

"But we agreed that he deserved it, didn't we, Hannah?" Crutchfield noted before turning to Jessie. "After all, Robbie was a very bad boy. He liked to touch children in wrong ways. He won't be doing that anymore."

Jessie let his words sink in. She had no idea whether Robert Rylance was really a pedophile. But it was clear that he'd told Hannah the man was. Her heart sank at the thought. Whether it was true or not, his goal was clear. He had kidnapped this man, told Hannah about his supposed crimes, and attempted to convince her that his killing was justified. He might have even tried to get her to do it. He was clearly trying to indoctrinate her in his ways. The question was, had he been successful?

"Bolton, I see that you've been busy with your lesson plan," Jessie said, trying again. "But maybe it's time to let Hannah leave to do some field study, see how she does on her own? You and I can stay here and chat about nature versus nurture and all that good stuff. What do you say?"

"That is a lovely offer, Miss Jessie," he replied, even as he stiffened his grip on Hannah and pushed the knife more firmly against her skin. "But I don't think we're to that point yet. She's still got some homework to do."

Jessie sensed him tiring of their banter and decided to switch things up to keep him off balance.

"You know, Bolton. I have to tell you I've had my fill of sharp objects pressed against throats for one day. Maybe we could take it down a notch here?"

Crutchfield smiled.

"I have to admit you've piqued my interest, Miss Jessie. You know I love to follow your exploits. But I'm ashamed to say I haven't been able to keep up with the details of your latest case, what with all my responsibilities here. But I look forward to reading about it in the paper later."

"Why wait? I'm happy to chew the fat about it now," she told him.

"I'm afraid that won't be possible," he said, feigning disappointment. "You see, I checked your special friend Ryan's call log and saw that he reached out to the local authorities. I'd imagine they're quite close now. Even with our unique hiding place here, I have to assume they'll be coming by soon. So there's no time for war stories, you see. We have to get right to the main event."

"What's that?" Jessie asked, projecting a confidence she didn't feel.

"You don't know yet, Miss Jessie?" he asked. "But I assumed you would have figured it out by now. Why do you think I permitted Miss Hannah's LinkedIn message to be sent when I could have easily deleted it? It's because I knew you'd come running. And I knew you wouldn't come with much backup for fear of making me act rashly. You'd come alone or at the most with your good buddy lying there. For someone who reads people for a living, you're quite easy to read yourself, Miss Jessie. I knew you'd come. I knew we'd be in this room together, where you would face judgment for your sins."

Jessie's pulse quickened at his words. She wasn't sure what he was getting at, but it was clear that he'd been planning this for some time. When she didn't respond, he continued.

"You're supposed to ask, 'what sins?', Miss Jessie. Come on now, keep up."

"I'm sure you'll tell me," she said sharply.

"Not me. That's the job for the judge," he said, his gaze turning away from her and toward the girl he was clutching. "Are you ready to pass judgment, Miss Hannah?"

And then, to Jessie's shock, he released the girl from his grip. Rather than run, she stood there, her eyes clear and her expression calm.

"I am," she said.

CHAPTER THIRTY FOUR

Jessie's stomach did a flip.

Hannah took a step away from Crutchfield, nodded at him and turned to face Jessie.

"Jessie Hunt, you are to be judged for your crimes, specifically for your deception and abandonment."

"What?" Jessie asked disbelievingly.

"Silence!" Crutchfield shouted. "Do not interrupt the judge while she passes sentence."

Jessie looked from him back to Hannah, who stared back at her impassively.

"Bolton told me your secret, Jessie," she said accusingly, her voice gaining strength with each word. "But it's really our secret, isn't it? He told me that the man who tortured me and killed my parents—the people who adopted and raised me—was my father. He also told me that this man, the man you killed in front of me, was your father too. He told me we're sisters. Is that true?"

Jessie wasn't sure what was happening or what Crutchfield had in mind. But she knew one thing—lying to Hannah now was not an option. She should have told her the truth a long time ago. She would do it now.

"Yes, Hannah," she said quietly. "Xander Thurman, the man who killed your parents in front of you, who did the same to my mother when I was a child, was my father and yours too. We're half-sisters."

No one spoke for several seconds. Jessie could feel Crutchfield drinking in the moment.

"But you never told me," Hannah finally said, an edge in her voice. "Not at the time. And not later when you came to see me at the foster home."

"No. I didn't know at first, certainly not when we faced Xander together. But I did know the truth when I visited you. I wanted to say something, but I was ordered not to by my superiors. I wasn't even supposed to see you until they gave approval. Still, looking back, I should have told you anyway. You deserved to know."

Hannah looked over at Crutchfield, who nodded for her to go on. She did.

"Don't you think," she demanded, her voice rising in anger, "that in the middle of the lowest point in my life, I would have wanted to know I had a sister, that I still had some kind of family?"

"Of cour—"

"Shut up," Hannah cut her off. "You chose to follow orders rather than reach out to your own flesh and blood. You left me to face the nightmares alone when you could have been there for me. You abandoned me. What kind of family does that?"

"Someone who needs to do better," Jessie conceded.

"Someone who's not really family," Crutchfield volunteered, his eyes gleaming greedily. "Someone who needs to face the consequences of her inaction. Don't you agree, Miss Hannah?"

"I do," she said forcefully, her whole body shaking with rage.

"It sounds like a verdict has been reached in this matter," Crutchfield said. "I think it's time for sentencing."

And then, to Jessie's astonishment, he handed Hannah the knife.

She reached out and took it, grasping the handle uncertainly in her hand. She looked hesitant, unsure what to do next.

"It's time, Miss Hannah," Crutchfield cooed. "Go ahead. Mete out the justice you deserve."

Jessie watched as the indecision drained from Hannah's face, replaced now by a grimace of conviction.

"Jessie Hunt," she said, loud and clear, using the same formal tone as earlier. "For the crimes of deception and abandonment, for choosing secrecy over family, for failing to protect your one living relative, I sentence you to death."

She took a step forward. Crutchfield leaned in, like he was watching a good movie. Jessie's mind flailed. She had no idea how to react. Was she supposed to fight a seventeen-year-old girl—her own flesh and blood—who'd been brainwashed into believing she was the enemy? Could she somehow wrestle the knife away from Hannah and turn it on Crutchfield? She waited for her brain to offer a suggestion, but nothing came.

Hannah looked down at the knife and fiddled clumsily with the grip. She turned to Crutchfield questioningly.

"Is this the best way to hold it?" she asked, extending it to show him.

"Grip it firmly," he said, moving forward. "But not too tight."

"Like this?" she asked, clasping it more confidently.

"Yes, that's . . ." he started to say.

But before he could finish the sentence, Hannah lunged forward, plunging the knife into the center of his stomach. Crutchfield stumbled back, gasping. Hannah leapt away from him, nearly tripping.

Almost immediately, before Jessie could fully process what was happening, Crutchfield ripped the knife from his own abdomen and advanced on her sister. He was raising it above his head when Jessie's brain and body finally seemed to reawaken.

She dove at Crutchfield, slamming into him and sending them both sprawling onto the dirt basement floor. Jessie landed hard on her side and felt a stinging sensation in her right rib. Before even looking up to get her bearings, she yelled.

"Run, Hannah!"

As she regrouped, she was relieved to hear feet rushing up the stairs. Looking up, she saw Crutchfield getting to his feet as well. He still had the knife in his hand and took a wild swing at Jessie.

She jumped away. As she did, she stepped on something and tumbled backward to the ground. It took her a second to realize that she'd fallen on the unconscious Ryan and the dead body of Robert Rylance.

For a second it looked like Crutchfield might come after her. But then she saw something click in his eyes. He turned and climbed the stairs, clearly laboring due to his stab wound. It only took a moment for her to realize what he was doing.

She scrambled to her feet and reached the bottom of the stairs as Crutchfield slammed the basement door shut. She was midway up when she heard it lock. By the time she got to the top, she had a full head of steam and threw herself against it. The door didn't budge. She tried again, this time rearing back and kicking the door. It didn't even rattle.

She stopped and listened. She could still hear Crutchfield as he lumbered away from the kitchen in the direction of the front door. As the sound of his movements faded away, she ignored the thumping of her heart beating in her eardrums and tried to focus.

How do I get out of here?

And then it hit her—the window. She hurried back down the stairs. For the first time, she noticed the shackles attached to a wooden post in the middle of the room. That must have been how he kept Hannah from attempting what she was about to try.

But when she ran over to the window, she realized there was another reason Hannah couldn't have gotten out. The small opening was at least nine feet above the ground, too far to reach for either of them. It might be possible to squeeze through if she could reach it, but she couldn't jump that high.

She looked back at the room, desperate for anything that might help. That's when her eyes fell on the chair still strapped to Rylance's dead body. Hannah must not have considered it an option. Or maybe she was too horrified at the idea of having to extricate it from a dead man surrounded by blood. Jessie had no such reservations.

She hurried over and began ripping the ropes from his body until she could pull the chair away. As she did, she looked at Ryan in the dim light, getting to evaluate him for the first time. He was breathing, his chest rising and falling slowly. There were no obvious wounds on him. She didn't know if he'd been drugged or hit on the head but at least for now, he was alive.

She debated trying to undo the ties around his wrists and ankles. But unlike the ropes attached to Rylance, they were plastic and she had nothing to cut them with. Besides, the time it would take was time she wasn't saving Hannah. She'd have to leave him for now. She did check to see if his extra pistol was still in his ankle holster but, as she expected, it was missing.

When she got Rylance's ropes loose, she grabbed the chair, letting the man's body thump unceremoniously to the ground. She darted back to the window, placed it underneath, and stepped up. She was now at eye level with the glass. It was smeared and dirty, making the neon pinks and blues of the strip club sign look like some cheap version of the aurora borealis.

Without hesitation, she bent her elbow and smashed it through the glass. Using the same technique, she knocked away the remaining shards lingering around the edges. Even after that, there were still a few jagged spots, but she didn't have time to worry about them.

She grabbed the outside of the window frame and yanked herself up and forward, ignoring the pain she felt as her right thigh was punctured and torn by something sharp.

Just another scar to add to the list.

She pulled herself through and pushed herself up onto all fours. From that vantage point, she looked out to see if she could catch a glimpse of either Hannah or Crutchfield. The former was nowhere to be found. But after a second to orient herself, she did catch sight of a slow-moving figure stumbling away from her, just passing the barn. It was Crutchfield.

Jessie scrambled to her feet and was about to chase after him when she had an idea. She scanned the area in front of the house. There on the ground where she'd left them, were both her guns and her phone. She was just starting to make her way over to them when the neon light from the strip club sign abruptly shut off, indicating that the club must be closed for the night.

Jessie stood there in the sudden darkness, unsure how to proceed. She was only about fifteen feet from her weapons. But in the pitch blackness, it might take several minutes of crawling on the ground to find her weapon, minutes she didn't have.

But then it occurred to her that she didn't need to crawl at all.

"Hey, Siri," she said as loudly as she dared, and when she heard the familiar "beep-beep," added, "Turn on my flashlight."

"It's on," the robotic female voice said as a bright light erupted from the phone, just ahead and to the left.

She rushed over, grabbed both her weapons, turned off the light, and began running in the direction she'd last seen Crutchfield. Her eyes were adjusting to the lack of light. It wasn't as dark as it had first seemed. Some of the houses had porch lights and the streetlights in the distance offered some guidance.

As she tore off after Crutchfield, she thought she could see what looked like flashing police lights approaching. To her amazement, it seemed that Chief Stoller had heeded Ryan's request and kept the sirens off.

She was just approaching the edge of the neighborhood, where it met the massive strip club parking lot. As she passed by the home closest to the lot, she saw him. Crutchfield was about twenty feet ahead of her, hobbling along, his head swiveling back and forth as he scanned the mostly empty lot for Hannah, who was nowhere to be found.

Jessie was about to hurry after him when she heard a sound.

"Psst," a soft voice hissed.

She turned around to see Hannah crouched by that first house, hiding behind a sad excuse for a hedge.

"Are you okay?" she whispered as she holstered her gun and approached the girl.

"No," Hannah replied quietly. "Not even close."

Jessie was about to respond when she saw Hannah's eyes open wide. She turned around and saw what had caused the reaction. Bolton Crutchfield had turned around and was now heading back in their direction. Maybe it was the police lights that made him change direction or maybe he'd heard the two of them talking.

Whatever the reason, he was moving straight toward them. As he came at them, his pace quickened and he lifted the hunting knife, which gleamed in the advancing police lights.

Jessie unholstered her gun and pointed it at the man, who was now less than ten feet from them.

"Stop," she yelled, her voice echoing through the night.

But he kept coming. So, she took a quick breath, exhaled, and fired. She was aiming for his chest, but with all the chaos and adrenaline, she instead hit him in the right hip. He took another step and stumbled, his right knee hitting the dirt, though he didn't go down completely. He was kneeling only half a dozen feet away now, almost close enough to touch. The knife was still in his hand.

"You shot me, Miss Jessie," he said through gritted teeth. "I wouldn't have thought you had it in you, though I appreciate that you only winged me."

"I was aiming for your heart," she said through gritted teeth.

A sense of clarity had come over her, one that she hadn't felt in a long time. She barely heard it when the approaching police vehicles in the parking lot turned on their sirens.

"Oh my," he said. "Does that mean you changed your mind at the last second? Or just that you're a bad shot?"

"Drop the knife, Bolton," Jessie said steadily, refusing to play his game. "Your wounds aren't life-threatening. You can surrender, go to a hospital, and end up in another psychiatric prison in a few months. Maybe you can even try to escape again."

"Look at you," he said, every word a strain. "Trying to be a professional to the last when, by all rights, you should be unloading a clip in me. What did I ever do to deserve such mercy?"

"I haven't forgotten how you helped me," she said quietly. "On cases, and when my father came after me. You warned me. I might not be here now if you hadn't. So, despite everything you've done, I want to give you the chance to turn yourself in. You've earned that. But I'm only offering once."

Crutchfield glanced back at the nearly one dozen police vehicles in the lot behind him, at the stream of officers pouring out of the cars with their weapons drawn, and then returned his attention to Jessie.

"What a disappointing outcome this is," he said ruefully, turning his attention to Hannah. "I had so hoped that you and I could plot a fresh course together. Now I fear that you'll have to go it alone, without an experienced guiding hand. How will you navigate the vagaries of your burgeoning talents without a mentor, I wonder? You are a squire without a knight, an apprentice without a master. It will be difficult for you, my dear."

"Drop the knife," Jessie repeated, keeping her gun trained on him, sensing that he had one last card he intended to play.

Out of the corner of her eye, she glanced over at Hannah to see if Crutchfield's words were having any impression on her. But the girl was staring back at him with an expression of revulsion and fury on her face.

"And as for you, Miss Jessie, my fears are different. I worry that you will never move past the pain that has haunted you since childhood. I worry that you will never truly love or accept love. I worry that the fear and mistrust that have dominated your life will continue to do so, that they will define you. I worry that you will die as an empty husk, calcified by bitterness and trauma. I fear it won't be pretty."

"It's a risk I'm willing to take," she said.

He looked at her, his cunning brown eyes boring into hers, and she knew what was coming. It was inevitable now.

"But I'm not," he said.

As he spoke, he pushed up from his kneeling position and threw himself at her. Anticipating his move, Jessie fired, this time hitting him square in the chest. She got off two more shots as he fell backward. As he landed, the knife dropped from his hand.

She stepped quickly toward him and kicked it away. As she holstered her gun, she bent down next to him. His chest was rising and falling quickly and his lips were moving as if he was trying to tell her something. She leaned in. But by the time she got close enough to hear him, Crutchfield's lips had gone still. His chest sank and didn't rise again. His darting eyes stopped and dimmed.

"Place your weapon on the ground, stand up, and step away," she heard a voice order through a bull horn.

Jessie looked up and, seeing close to two dozen guns pointed in her general direction, did as she was instructed. She slowly got to her feet, taking several steps away from the body and raising her hands above her head. Hannah emerged from behind the hedge and did the same. Jessie glanced over at the girl and tried to smile.

"It's over," she assured her. "It's finally over."

Hannah shook her head.

"It's never over."

CHAPTER THIRTY FIVE

They shared the same ambulance.

But before that, Ryan was taken separately in his own and immediately transported to Redlands Community Hospital, the closest option. He was conscious but generally unresponsive as he was wheeled into the vehicle. Jessie promised him that she'd meet him at the hospital.

As his ambulance pulled away, Chief Stoller waddled over with a legitimately chastened expression on his face.

"I'm thinking maybe I owe you an apology," he said under his breath.

As she stared him down, she thought of a lot of things she owed *him*, including a good beat-down. But she was too tired to say that, much less actually deliver one.

"Thank you," she said instead, ultimately deciding that alienating the guy served no useful purpose. If she ever had another case in the area, she knew exactly who to call for a favor.

Since neither she nor Hannah had life-threatening injuries, both were patched up and remained at the scene briefly to answer investigators' questions and guide them through the house. But after about twenty minutes, Jessie saw Hannah starting to shake. Fearing she was going into shock, she told the detectives they could finish their questioning at the hospital and asked the EMTs to take them to the same one Ryan was sent to.

"I'm sorry," she said again. "I should have told you the truth that day on the porch."

Hannah, who was lying on a stretcher with a thermal blanket wrapped around her, nodded.

"It's okay. I wish you had. But the truth is, I only pretended to be so pissed to trick Bolton. I needed him to trust me so I could get close enough to . . . do what I did."

"You were very convincing," Jessie said, trying to hide just how unsettled she was by Hannah's performance.

"Yeah, well, my life depended on it. Both of ours did, I guess."

"I guess so," Jessie agreed. "You know, this is the second time I wouldn't have made it if you weren't around."

"That's one way to look at it," Hannah replied. "Another way is that you never would have been in danger either time if it wasn't for me."

Jessie smiled.

"I guess this means we should stick together," she said, "so we can have each other's back."

Hannah smiled back as she settled onto the stretcher.

"I'd like that," she said, sighing deeply.

Before Jessie could respond, the girl had fallen asleep.

She was too amped to do the same, so she simply scooted over closer to her half-sister and rested her hand on the younger girl's. She left it there the whole ride.

Two hours later, Jessie stepped out of Ryan's hospital room to take the phone call from Garland Moses.

The detective had woken up briefly, long enough to ask what had happened, and look relieved at the outcome. Then he'd sunk back into a drug-aided slumber. He sounded like himself but the doctor said he'd been hit in the back of the head with something heavy and, though there didn't seem to be any internal bleeding, they wanted to keep him under observation for several days to make sure he really was okay. They said he might be in and out of it for at least the next twelve hours.

Hannah was asleep one floor up. The medical staff had sedated her and treated the shackle wounds on her wrists and ankles while she slept. They expected she'd wake up around early afternoon. Considering that it was approaching 5 a.m., that didn't seem nearly long enough.

The nurse had offered to give Jessie something to help her sleep as well. But she declined, wanting to stay awake and clear-headed in case either Ryan or Hannah stirred. She did accept pain medication for the shoulder and rib she'd bruised while attacking Crutchfield in the basement. And they'd numbed up her thigh nicely so they could stitch it up where the glass cut her open when she climbed through the basement window. It was only eleven stitches, which seemed like nothing to her anymore.

When the call from Garland came, she was reviewing the Redlands detectives' preliminary report and riding the residual wave of pain meds. From their search of Robert Rylance's home laptop, it looked like Crutchfield's pedophilia claims about him had proven true. With great reluctance, she got up and walked into the hall.

"Hi, Garland," she said, forcing some semblance of peppiness into her tone. "How's it going?"

"How are you?" he asked, sounding slightly less gruff than usual.

"Oh, you know how it goes. Shoot a serial killer, find your missing half-sister, watch your... colleague almost die. Busy evening, I'd say."

"I heard you were injured," he said, not reacting to her gallows humor.

"Nothing major," she answered, dropping the act. "A few stitches and some bruises. I'm used to far worse. They actually officially released me but I'm sticking around to keep an eye on Hannah and Detective Hernandez."

"How are they?"

"Ryan got a bad bonk on the head. They're going to keep him here until they're sure he's good. Hannah's okay physically. But I'm not sure about psychologically. She's been through so much, including serving as a human experiment for a serial killer. I'm going to see if she can stay with me so I can keep an eye on her."

"That's not a bad idea. You should also get her in to see someone ASAP," Garland suggested.

"I actually already had someone in mind. My therapist, Janice Lemmon, knows the whole back story. She could hit the ground running in the first session."

"Ah, yes," Garland said warmly. "I know Janice well. She's an excellent choice."

Something in his tone made Jessie wonder just *how* well he knew Dr. Janice Lemmon.

"I feel like maybe I suddenly know more about you than I'm comfortable with," Jessie said teasingly.

"I contain multitudes, Hunt," he said cryptically.

"Apparently so," she agreed, then added, "Thank you, by the way."

"For what?"

"For the lead on Rylance, which led me to Hannah and Crutchfield. I realize you took a risk passing that along to me, even if it was in coded form."

"I have no idea what you're talking about, Hunt," he said, borderline convincingly.

"Of course you don't," she replied, smiling to herself. "Does that mean you won't be sharing how you made the connection between Rylance and Crutchfield?"

"Well, I'll let you go, Hunt," he said, ignoring her question. "I just wanted to check in with you and see how you were doing now that it's finally over."

"I'm good, thanks," she assured him. "Thanks for checking in. I'll see you soon."

She hung up and returned to Ryan's room, where she settled back in the uncomfortable chair that had been her home base for the last hour. She wanted to go back to reviewing the detectives' report but something Garland had said was eating at her, something about checking in now that it was over.

She turned it over in her head for a minute before she realized that it wasn't Garland Moses's comment that was bouncing around in her head. It was something Hannah had said, something that didn't fully register in the moment she'd said it. But now it did.

It's never over.

Now Available for Pre-Order!

BLAKE PIERCE

THE PERFECT AFFAIR
(A Jessie Hunt Psychological Suspense Thriller–Book Seven)

"A masterpiece of thriller and mystery. Blake Pierce did a magnificent job developing characters with a psychological side so well described that we feel inside their minds, follow their fears and cheer for their success. Full of twists, this book will keep you awake until the turn of the last page."
—Books and Movie Reviews, Roberto Mattos (re *Once Gone*)

THE PERFECT AFFAIR is book #7 in a new psychological suspense series by bestselling author Blake Pierce, whose #1 bestseller *Once Gone* (a free download) has over 1,000 five-star reviews.

A porn star is found dead, and the LAPD doesn't think much of it. But FBI agent Jessie Hunt, 29, senses something much more sinister at play, something that may just reach into the upper echelons of power and society.

A fast-paced psychological suspense thriller with unforgettable characters and heart-pounding suspense, THE PERFECT AFFAIR is book #7 in a riveting new series that will leave you turning pages late into the night.

Book #8 in the Jessie Hunt series will be available soon.

THE PERFECT AFFAIR
(A Jessie Hunt Psychological Suspense Thriller—Book Seven)

Did you know that I've written multiple novels in the mystery genre? If you haven't read all my series, click the image below to download a series starter!

Made in the USA
Coppell, TX
12 January 2022

71453738R00121